CHRISTMAS AT THE WINTER PALACE: A LADY OF THE COURT, THE CHRISTMAS GIFT: 2-IN-1 NOVELLA COLLECTION

KATHRYN CUSHMAN

Seventh Pew Press

A LADY OF THE COURT

To Lisa Cushman—you've spent years smiling and nodding politely while I droned on and on about 18th century Russia. The fact that you were willing to accompany me halfway around the world so I could do research is beyond amazing. Covid may have gotten the last laugh on that one, but the fact that you were willing to go means more than you will ever know. Thanks for the encouragement and laughs along the way.

CHAPTER 1

November 1750
Kazan, Russia

*A*lyona Arkadyevna Balashova could not breathe.

She stretched out her hand toward Svetlana, but before she reached her, dark blotches erupted between them. The world tilted and the floor came flying toward her face. The room went black.

"Mistress! Mistress!" The voice floated above her, muffled and thick, and barely discernible. Something tugged at her back, and then whatever had been crushing her ribs was removed. "Can you hear me?" The words became clearer. "Can you open your eyes?"

Somehow Alyona managed to pry her lids apart. The room wobbled around her, and suddenly Svetlana's face appeared near hers. Very near. "Speak to me. Please speak to me. Oh, please do not be dead."

Alyona blinked a few times and attempted to push Svetlana away. "I am fine." The labored words required all her strength.

"Are you truly?" Svetlana sat back and placed both hands

over her face, shaking her head back and forth while peering out through her fingers. "You do not look fine. No, no, you do not." She leaned closer. "You look dreadful."

Alyona attempted to sit up, but her vision blurred and she fell back. "What happened?"

"I almost killed you, is what. Oh, just think what His Excellency would have done to me if he had arrived and found you dead. Oh, just think." Svetlana began to sob hysterically.

In spite of her wooziness, Alyona forced herself to sit up and hug the poor thing. How she did like to carry on. "There, there now. I am quite alive as you can see."

Svetlana wiped her eyes, but the sobs did not cease. "He would have killed me, too, yes he would."

As her dizziness abated, Alyona's annoyance with Svetlana grew. "No more of that. No one is going to kill you." She managed to push herself to her feet. "Now, let's try again."

Svetlana, still sitting on the floor, scooted backwards. "I couldn't. What if it happens again?"

"Do not make an elephant out of a fly. All is well. We will not go so tight this time."

"I told you it was too tight before, didn't I? You didn't listen to me then, and you won't listen to me now. You will die, and His Excellency will see to it that I also die when he returns and finds you dead. I will not touch it. I will not."

"Then I suppose I shall be forced to go downstairs and ask Sergei to help me."

"You wouldn't." Svetlana clapped her hand across her mouth, perfectly scandalized, as had been the intention.

"It would appear that I have no other choice. My father will be arriving within the hour, and if you are not willing to lace my corset, then I shall have to find someone else to do it. The goal is to surprise him when he sees me in my new ball gown, not surprise him by finding me half naked."

Svetlana shook her head. "Please do not make me do it."

"We must perfect this before I leave for Moscow. It is one thing to faint in my own bedchamber; it would be quite another to pass out in a crowded ballroom."

A Moscow ballroom! Just the thought made her want to shout. To sing. To dance. And dance. And dance. And dance and dance and dance.

Svetlana sighed, her defeat certain. She pointed toward the corset, which now hung loose around Alyona's waist. "I told you when this thing arrived that it was much too fine to be hidden under a dress. It's jinxed, that's what it is. Jinxed, jinxed, jinxed."

Alyona looked down at the green silk with an inwrought floral pattern. "It does seem like a waste of such lovely fabric, doesn't it? Still, Tutor always says 'nothing is wasted if it makes you feel good.' And I must admit, just knowing I'm wearing something this beautiful makes me feel amazing." Alyona twirled around and threw her hands in the air.

Svetlana snorted. "There is not a corset in all of the Russias that could make me feel amazing, even one as pretty as this." She shook her head vigorously. "No, no, no."

"Then it's a good thing that I am the one who will be attending the balls." Alyona rubbed her fingertips across the embroidered silk. Did other young ladies in Moscow wear such beautiful corsets on a daily basis? St. Petersburg, too? She sighed with happiness at the very thought of such things.

"They say all the ladies at court are shaped like cones, they are laced up so tight." Svetlana patted her hips through the yards of flowing fabric of her sarafan—a plain brown fabric dress fitted at the chest, then wide and voluminous to the ground. "Makes me thankful to be a servant, not a great lady."

"As you are counting that particular blessing, please do what you must to get me cone shaped, preferably while I'm still able to draw breath." Alyona laughed as she turned, then remembered herself and attempted to speak in her most glamorous voice. "Now lace it up tight, but do be careful."

The ladies at court. Alyona could hardly wait to see exactly how they looked, how they spoke, how they styled their hair. After years of listening to her friend Roza prattle on and on about it, she would finally get the experience herself.

As the laces tightened, the whalebone stays pushed into her skin. When it reached the point where it hurt to inhale, she said, "I believe that is enough."

Svetlana tied it off, then circled around her, as if to confirm that Alyona was still conscious. "Yes. You are cone shaped. You are, yes, yes." She gazed toward the mirror. "My sarafan is awfully plain, isn't it?" She drew out the skirt and sighed.

"It is lovely because you are wearing it, and you are lovely."

Svetlana's cheeks turned pink at the compliment. She released the fabric from between her fingers. "Am not."

The truth was, her lady's maid was lovely in a most unusual sort of way. She was tiny in every respect. The top of her head did not rise to Alyona's shoulders, her arms were stick thin, and her face all angles and points. It gave her an almost fairy-like appearance. All she needed was a set of wings.

"You most certainly are. Every girl in Russia wishes she had your huge blue eyes. As for fashion, what about the red sarafan you are preparing for Christmas morning? The embroidered skirt is gorgeous. I bet even the empress herself would approve."

Svetlana shrugged. "I doubt that very much. Did you hear what they say about her? She never wears the same dress twice. Never, never."

"I have heard that, as well."

"And she doesn't allow sarafans at all." Svetlana made a *tsking* sound. "I bet she has never been comfortable a single day in her life. Not one."

In truth, Empress Elizabeth's father, Peter the Great, had

outlawed traditional Russian clothing for the nobles, requiring instead that they dress in the European fashion. All part of his efforts to show the world that his country was not some uneducated backwater. As current ruler, Empress Elizabeth was less stringent about this rule, but traditional dresses were frowned upon, definitely at court—or so they said. The upcoming ball in Moscow was to be Alyona's first foray into society. Just one more month!

"I wonder what your mother would have thought about all this."

Her mother. Alyona's memories of her mother had grown a bit dimmer over the past couple of years, but not the pain of her loss. "She would have been happy. It was always her wish for me to be presented at court. That's why she insisted on hiring tutors on every subject from science, to art, to French. She wanted me to be fully prepared when the time came."

"Yet she often wore sarafans, and she never went to balls."

The words twisted like a knot in Alyona's chest. Her mother's lowly birth and her father's loss of inheritance and title because he chose to marry her were not matters Alyona cared to discuss, especially with her young maid. "She wanted this for me. She always said so."

"Cook says she always fretted that she had caused such an upset in your father's life. She wanted you to be able to choose your own path. She did, yes."

"Enough of this talk. Rather than speculating about what we do not know, we must prepare for what is ahead."

The series of winter balls in Moscow were to be preparation for the upcoming summer season, when her father would conduct her to the Catherine Palace in Tsarskoe Selo. For the entire summer season! For now, they would attend several grand Moscow balls, which were scheduled before the forty days of the Nativity Fast.

Svetlana dropped the pannier over Alyona's head and slid it

down around her hips. "They say that at her royal balls, the empress sends servants through the crowd with ink to stamp the dresses of all who attend, so that no gown can be worn twice to one of her events. Never worn twice. Can you believe it?"

Although Alyona loved new gowns, when she thought about the serfs living nearby who could barely keep their families warm and fed through the winter, the rumors of this kind of extravagance did bother her. She was more than certain that it was just small-town gossip and looked forward to the day that she returned triumphant and announced they'd all been wrong. "I must see it for myself before I believe it." Alyona glanced out the window.

A dark figure was racing up the road. "What is that?" She made out the form of a cloaked man on a black horse in full gallop, clouds of snow flying up behind its hooves. "Surely that's not Father home already."

Svetlana walked to the window. "It's not like your father to ride in so fast. He usually enjoys a saunter, captains by his side, so everyone has a chance to notice."

As much as Alyona loved her father, she was not blind to his weaknesses. What Svetlana said was true enough. Father usually returned from his trips perched upon his saddle, parading through town with his stallion at a walk so that all could see and admire him, the medals on his chest, and the cut of his uniform. Arkady Alexandrovich Balashov was one of the most decorated generals in all of Russia, and he enjoyed the fact that everyone knew it.

They lived in the city of Kazan, which was becoming a leading center of trade, and it was in the interest of the empire to keep it protected. His talent served well here, and Empress Elizabeth rewarded him amply. This post also served to keep his gruff demeanor and quick temper in Kazan, far away from court where the empress preferred more of a timid and ingratiating presence. Or so Father had always said. Alyona could not wait to find out for herself.

In her most recent wagonload of gifts, the empress had sent the usual exotic spices and European wines, but this time she had also included several bolts of fine silk and velvet meant especially for Alyona, as well as the finely embroidered corset now cinched tight around her waist. These would provide her a wardrobe fit for court.

For years, she had listened to the stories from Roza, whose father was a count. Her family had been going to Tsarskoe Selo for the summer season for years, and oh the stories she would tell about thick crystal, exotic animals, and handsome men dressed in fine suits. Last year, she had met and married Baron Gorbunov and was now a baroness. Just imagine! She wrote glowing letters of life at the theater and fine parties. It all sounded so exotic and romantic. If only Alyona could find true love in the midst of it all, she knew that her every dream would come true.

"Move away, mistress. You'll be seen and you're not half-dressed, no you are not."

Alyona backed away from the window, but Svetlana moved closer and continued to watch. She expelled a sigh. "It's not His Excellency, thanks be to God. He would be angry if he arrived before you were ready to greet him." She made an exaggerated shivering motion. "Oh that man and his tempers. Best to avoid them. Yes. Yes."

"That is true enough. Help me lift this gown over my head and let's finish my hair before he really does arrive. He will accuse us of sloth if he finds me unmade."

Svetlana moved toward her. "Oh, we don't want to get him started on one of those lectures, that much is certain. Yes. We must hurry." She made quick work of securing the pannier, and in her haste she even refrained from her usual comments about how strange it was that fancy women would want to make their hips look so wide. She picked up the gown, the silver embroidery gleaming on the heavy white velvet. "I wonder if we should have used gold embroidery instead. It would bring out the copper highlights in your light brown hair, which are so pretty and unusual. But then I think silver is better because it sets off the pale blue of your eyes." Svetlana arranged the dress over the pannier. "Your father will pop his buttons when he sees you."

"I do hope he likes it." A frisson of excitement tickled her spine. She wanted to squeal but remembered that she must be dignified now that she was to be a lady. "I trust that Cook remembered to prepare all of his favorites for today?"

Svetlana snorted. "Believe me, she remembered. No one wants to start out on your father's bad side after he returns home."

"Svetlana, you must stop making that sound. You know how it annoys Father."

"Annoys him. Yes. You are right." She rubbed the back of her hand across her nose, then returned to her task of arranging the dress.

Father and his company had spent the past month traveling up the Volga River. Every year rumors of unrest and uprisings circulated, and every so often Father's company would travel out to assess the situation. These trips were mostly wasted, as Father always reported the stories to be "nothing more than babushka gossip." Still, Alyona knew he enjoyed the excuse to gad about the countryside, especially before the Christmas holidays when he'd be "cooped up with women and priests for far too long."

Still, Alyona knew without doubt that he loved nothing better than being home with her. He would sit for hours, listening each night as she read aloud after dinner—one of the many practices begun by her mother that Alyona now carried on in her absence.

As Svetlana began fastening the buttons with quick hands,

the sound of running feet pounded up the stairs. A quick knock came at the door.

"Go away," Svetlana shouted. "Mistress is still getting dressed."

The pounding continued. Svetlana abandoned her buttons and hurried to the door, eased it open only a sliver, and stuck her head out into the hallway. "I said, go away. Mistress is getting—" She paused for a moment as frantic whispers came from the outside. "But how?" More whispers.

Alyona moved forward so she could hear what was being said. Svetlana closed the door and leaned against it. "Oh, mistress." Her hand pressed against her chest as she took deep breaths.

"What is it? What has happened?"

"It's your father."

Alyona moved closer. "What about my father?"

"He has taken ill."

Father ill? In all of her life, Alyona had never witnessed such a thing. While she'd watched her mother battle ailments over the years, especially the last bout of pneumonia that had finally claimed her, she had never seen her father so much as sneeze. "Will he be arriving soon? We must prepare his room as best we can."

Svetlana's eyes went wide. "He is not coming here. He is too sick to move."

"Then we must go to him. Help me out of this dress. We must prepare for travel immediately."

Once again, Svetlana shook her head. "No, mistress, no. Your father is being well tended."

"And he will be even more so once we arrive." She turned so Svetlana could undo the buttons.

She made no move to do so. "He has forbidden it."

Alyona wanted to grab the girl and shake her, but she managed to refrain. "Enough of that. Of course we are going."

She held up her hair, but Svetlana still did not touch the buttons.

"He said you must not mar your beautiful face."

Alyona could contain herself no longer. She whirled around, grabbed Svetlana by the shoulders, and glared down at her. "Stop all this nonsense and help me. Tending him will by no means mar my face."

"Yes, it would, yes, yes." Svetlana made the sign of the cross before she spoke again. "It's smallpox."

CHAPTER 2

*O*utside the well-traveled roads of Kazan, the snow grew deeper and heavier with each sinking step. Alyona trudged forward, determined to continue no matter how difficult. Her father was many versts away, and she had only herself to rely on. The household staff, without exception, had refused to help her.

So Alyona set out walking without looking back. They all expected her to become discouraged and return within the hour, but she would do no such thing.

Thankfully, it was a fine sunny day, without wind or falling snow. "Give thanks for the small things," her mother had always said. And she had given thanks for everything, including each sip of broth or water and each gasping breath before the lung infection had claimed her life. If Mamochka could be thankful for those things, then Alyona could certainly find reasons for gratitude now.

"Mistress." The boy's voice called from behind, but she did not turn. Instead, she concentrated on moving her feet forward. "Mistress." The voice grew closer, but there was no reason to stop. She had no intention of wasting good travel time with a pointless argument.

"Mistress, please." Tikhon, one of the grooms from the stable, huffed with exertion as he came up beside her.

"Tikhon, you are wasting time—yours and mine." She wrested her left foot from the snow, took the longest stride she could manage, then leaned forward as the foot sank deep into the next step. "I am going to my father regardless of what you might say. You may return to the house and tell the others you tried to stop me, but I would not be persuaded."

"I have come to tell you they are preparing the vozok for you and packing your trunk. Please, return to the house with me now. Everything will be ready for departure within an hour."

Alyona turned and looked at him doubtfully. "Truly?"

"Yes, Mistress. Cook herself demanded it."

Cook did more than prepare the meals. She also ruled the household with a stubbornness that rivaled Alyona's father. If she had decreed it… "You must promise me."

"I give you my tooth. Please, come back with me now, else I won't get my supper tonight."

Alyona considered this. The last part she knew to be true, so it made the rest of it easier to believe. "All right, then."

They began the long walk back, which was somewhat eased by the path they had already made through the deep snow. "Thank goodness I caught you when I did. I couldn't have run much farther." His words came out as foggy wheezes into the cold morning air.

When they arrived back at the house, Cook was overseeing the loading of provisions. She shook her head when Alyona approached. "This is madness. But since you will not be dissuaded, I prepared some food for you and some broth for your father."

"Thank you, Cook." Two trunks were carried out from the house and loaded onto the back of the vozok. Alyona turned to

Cook. "I do not need so much. Tending a sick man requires little."

Svetlana bounded out the door behind the men. "The smaller trunk is for me."

Alyona shook her head. "No. I must do this alone."

"And you shall do it alone, only I will be beside you. Yes. Yes."

"Absolutely not." Alyona waved her away. "I will not hear of it."

Cook placed her hands on each of Alyona's shoulders and stared her straight in the eye. "She is going. Your father will be furious that we allowed this, but if you traveled the distance alone"—she whistled— "none of us has the courage to face that."

"So...choose. Svetlana goes with you, or we put these horses away and you get back to your walking."

Knowing that argument would only serve to waste more time, Alyona finally agreed. "Will you see to it that the drivers have an extra set of warm gloves and hats for the journey?"

"Of course."

Normally while traveling by vozok, Alyona insisted that the drivers stop from time to time and come sit by the furnace inside to warm themselves. This journey could not spare time for such niceties.

She climbed into the vozok with Svetlana, and soon they were leaving the city behind. In spite of the fact that the specially made carriage contained a small furnace and extra-thick siding, as night fell she shivered under layers of fur blankets. Svetlana curled up in a tight ball and fell asleep, a luxury that eluded Alyona.

As morning's first rays shone from behind the rolling hills, they passed through a small village. It contained only a handful of old wooden storefronts, shuttered tight against the bitter cold. They drove past the shops and into a snow-covered landscape dotted with scattered small homesteads, with small barns and small storehouses. When they passed through the gates of a larger estate, she knew they had arrived at their destination.

The sick were being housed in the overseer's cottage. It was an old wooden building, but it appeared well kept. Plumes of dark smoke rose from all three chimneys.

"Wake up, Svetlana, we have arrived."

Her maid stirred and rubbed her eyes. When she realized where they were, she crossed herself, her hands trembling. Still, she stood and folded the blanket.

Alyona clasped her hand. "There is nothing you can do here. Return home with the vozok. I will remain until Father is well enough to travel, then send word when it is time to retrieve us. There is no need for you to tarry until then."

Svetlana shook her head. "If you are mad enough to do this, then I will be mad enough to do it with you. Besides, Cook would give me the rod if I returned without you."

This was true, but Alyona would find a way to fight it. She just hadn't thought of it yet. She climbed down from the vozok, pulling back her shoulders and preparing for what she was about to encounter.

The door of the cottage creaked open, and a woman wearing a worn black sarafan and headscarf came out to meet them. She was bone thin with a tired face full of crags that spoke of the hard life of a Russian serf. Her voice cracked with weariness. "This is a sick house. You must not enter here." Her eyes swept across Alyona's dress, then over her shoulder at Svetlana, who stood just behind.

Although Alyona wore her oldest travel clothes, she knew that to this serf woman, her blue wool dress still seemed very fine. The thought embarrassed her. "Yes, I am aware it is a sick house. My father is housed here. I have come to care for him."

"No. There are strict orders. I am not to allow anyone inside. Just the doctor and my sisters and me. It is not safe."

"It is not safe for you either, is it? And yet here you are."

"I am doing what I must. I have no other choice."

"If you, a stranger, have no other choice, then I, his daughter, have even less. His name is General Arkady Alexandrovich Balashov. Please take me to him at once."

Her eyes lit with recognition. "Your father is very ill. He will not know you."

Alyona nodded. "That is perhaps for the better. He would not be happy I am here."

"Of course not. You shouldn't be here. Besides, when he is awake, he is not happy about anything."

Svetlana snorted. "Nothing is new about that."

The woman ignored the outburst and continued to study Alyona. "If he would not wish it, then why have you come?"

"Because I will not leave my sick father to the care of strangers." She nodded toward the woman. "Not that I doubt your competence. Only that at the worst of times, it is better to be near those we love."

She squinted at Alyona, as if trying to understand what she was seeing. Finally, she said, "I must agree with that. I am only surprised that someone in your position feels that way."

"Then I apologize for those in my position who have acted in a way that would cause your doubt. What is your name?"

"Inna."

"Inna, if you would be so good as to take me to my father. And then could you possibly find a safe place for my maid, Svetlana, to stay? She insisted on making this journey with me, but I do not want her brought into danger because of her loyalty to me."

Svetlana crossed her arms. "As I have already said, if you are going to do this, so am I. Yes, I am."

"My father would be doubly unhappy to see both of us."

"Your father is doubly unhappy to see me on most days. I do

not believe that it should make much difference when he is sick. No, no."

Alyona looked again at Inna. "Please, if you could find a room for us," she turned again toward Svetlana, "you could go with our things, get it all arranged, and when I return to rest, it will comfort me to know that you are there to help."

"But I—"

"She is correct. The general has his own room, but it is very small. The two of you could scarce fit in there together." Inna extended a hand to stop Svetlana from advancing and turned her gaze upon Alyona, looking her directly in the eyes. "And when your mistress gets sick, and she will if she insists on coming in here," she said each word slowly, making certain that Alyona knew the full implications, "she will need you to take care of her."

"Mistress, please don't go."

Alyona pulled her sleeve away. "Enough of that."

Inna pointed to the top of the hill. "They will offer hospitality since you are the general's daughter. I will take your maid up there and secure a room."

A large manor in the old wooden style sprawled across the hilltop. Smoke curled from the chimneys, giving a warm and welcoming appearance. "Who lives there? Is it a family?"

"Yes. The master of the estate and his wife and five children."

Alyona shook her head. "It would not be right. If I should bring smallpox into their home...I could not bear it. Is there an outbuilding or a room in the barn where we might be allowed to stay?"

"It would not be acceptable."

"Nor would it be acceptable for us to risk an entire family for the sake of my comfort."

"You continue to surprise." Inna gestured toward the overseer's cottage. "Let me show you to your father, and then I will sort out a place for the two of you to lodge. Meanwhile, your maid should wait outside."

She opened the door and went inside. Alyona followed, dreading what she might find.

THE AIR IN THE COTTAGE STANK OF VOMIT AND sickness. In spite of the fact that morning had dawned, it was so dark that Alyona could see almost nothing save for the light of the Russian stove on the far wall. "We keep the windows covered with dark cloth. Light hurts their eyes," Inna whispered.

Alyona nodded her understanding, struggling not to gag at the horrible stench. As her eyes adjusted to the darkness, she could make out dark lumps that appeared to be about a half-dozen men lying on the floor along the far wall. The silence pressed against her, broken only by low moans that seemed to accompany the breathing of the man in the far corner.

Steam wafted from a large kettle, which likely held medicinal roots and herbs, but the air was so thick with smells, Alyona could not say for sure. Inna lit a small candle, using her left hand to block the light from shining in the direction of the sick men. "Follow me. Be mindful of your steps, the planks are uneven."

"Thank you." They made their way through the main room and down a dark hallway. Inna opened the last door on the right but then stopped without going inside. She stood, still and silent, far past the point Alyona could bear it.

"Let me pass."

Inna held up her hand to signal for quiet, but Alyona could wait no longer. "I said let me pass."

"There is no reason." Inna turned to look over her shoulder. "Your father is no longer here."

"What do you mean?" Alyona pushed Inna aside, which caused her to stumble as she entered the small room. She righted herself, realizing in the process that there was no sound. None at all. She could just make out her father's form lying on the small bed.

"Father, it's me. I'm here." She reached out to take his hand, but Inna jerked her back.

"Do not touch him. There is nothing you can do to help him now."

Inna reached over to the window and removed the dark cloth. A shaft of light landed on the bed where her father lay, his face so distorted by swollen pustules that she would not have recognized him.

Alyona fell to her knees beside the bed. "No, Father, no. Don't leave me. Please, you must fight. Please, Father, please. I need you." There had to be some mistake. Her father was strong, he was invincible. This swollen lump of a human—her father could not end this way. He just couldn't.

"You must go. Now." Inna reached under Alyona's arms, picked her up, and dragged her from the room, with Alyona kicking and fighting the entire way.

"No." She needed to get back to him. It was all a mistake. It had to be. "Let me go."

When they reached the front door, Inna jerked it open and pushed Alyona to the porch. "Now get out of here and stay out. Your father is gone. There is no reason for you to die, too."

Svetlana rushed over. "Mistress?"

Alyona grabbed Inna's arm. "Let me inside. I need to be with my father."

"Do you also need to die or be scarred for the rest of your life?"

"I don't care."

"Do you care about sentencing those who would tend you to the same fate?"

This thought stopped her. Svetlana stood by her side even now, eyes wide with fright. If Alyona got sick, Svetlana, Cook, and a whole house full of servants would tend her. How many of them might also become infected? How many of their family members?

Tears streamed down her cheeks. Finally, she nodded. "Yes, I shall go."

Inna said, "There's a wash house just over there. Go clean yourself and you should burn the dress you are wearing. Who knows what it might have touched."

And so it was that less than an hour after her arrival, Alyona was returning home—washed, in a different dress, her heart shattered beyond repair. How could this have happened? His strength had always been enough for both of them, for everyone. How were they supposed to carry on now?

She curled up in a ball and lay on the floor of the vozok, refusing to speak, for the entirety of the ride home.

CHAPTER 3

March 1752
Kazan, Russia

*W*ell over a year after her father's death, Alyona still fought the daily urge to remain in bed with the covers pulled over her head. She could not afford this luxury, as there was an estate to run and she was still on the learning end of how to manage any of it. They could not live indefinitely off her father's savings. Many lives depended on her, and she knew so little.

Rather than ring for her lady's maid, she removed one of her mother's old sarafans from the back of the wardrobe and dressed herself. She wrapped a thick wool shawl around her shoulders, made her way downstairs, and pulled on her oldest felt boots. They were stained and worn from many walks on the snowy lane.

The cold air stung her cheeks as she made her way outside, but she welcomed the feeling. She attempted to pray, the same as she did every morning, as she crunched through the snow, but it had begun to feel so hopeless. Once again, she returned to the house, having no clearer idea of what was to become of her. Of all of them.

She entered through the back door unnoticed. Perhaps a few minutes alone in her father's study, then she would summon Svetlana to help her prepare for the day ahead.

Just as Alyona grabbed the handle, Svetlana called from somewhere behind, "Mistress, do not go in th—"

The warning came too late, as the door opened to reveal Colonel Tchichagov, hands clasped behind his back, studying her father's favorite painting. He turned upon her entry and bowed in an exaggerated fashion. "Alyona Arkadyevna, I am glad they found you so quickly. Your servants are far less helpful than their station demands." He scowled toward the door, where Svetlana had rushed in behind her.

"The helpfulness of my servants is not your concern, sir."

Svetlana made a snorting sound, but Alyona pretended not to hear it. She just glared at the man in front of her. He wore a ridiculous wig, with powdered curls that framed his wrinkled forehead.

"Hmm. We shall see." He sank into the chair behind the desk—her father's chair—and rubbed his hands down the arms as if testing the quality of the leather. "I am glad to see you looking so..." he leaned forward, rested his elbows on the desk, then made a show of letting his gaze drift over her from head to toe—the old sarafan, the hair that had not yet been styled, "... well." He sniffed with unveiled condescension.

"Thank you." She would give his comment the benefit of no more words.

He was old and tired looking, but with the air of superiority of someone who had been considered special all of his life, even though he had done nothing to earn it. His birth into an aristocratic family with strong political connections was the only thing he could boast of. Father had never liked him.

He leaned back in the chair, tilting his chin a fraction higher. "I bring news."

"What news?"

"I have received a letter from the empress's secretary." He waited, clearly expecting a reaction to the fact that he was so important that the empress of all the Russias' secretary would write to him.

Since her father had received regular communication from the empress herself, this news did not in any way impress. However, as he seemed disinclined to leave until she acknowledged this grand achievement, she finally said, "I congratulate you, sir."

An interminable silence ensued. When she could bear it no longer, she said, "If there is nothing more, I will have my maid show you to the door. Perhaps you will find her more useful this time."

His face pinched in anger, giving the appearance of a rotten potato as it caved in upon itself. Rotten potatoes. Yes, this reminded her that the storehouse needed to be checked by the end of the day. There was much to do, and wasting time on this silly man would not facilitate that. She gestured toward the door, but still he did not stand.

"The empress has requested that you be conducted to St. Petersburg so you may fall under her personal care."

To be under the empress's personal care? In St. Petersburg? For a fraction of a second, Alyona allowed herself to experience the excitement—and relief—before reality stole it away. While she knew little about running estates, it was solely her presence —and the fact that she was the orphaned child of her beloved mother—that kept local merchants and even some of the servants from robbing them blind. If Alyona left, it would quickly fall apart. "This would not be an opportune time for me to be away."

He scoffed. "The empress of Russia has told you to come to St. Petersburg. There is no other choice for you. Her commands do not represent an option."

"He's right, mistress. I have heard the stories about the tongues she's cut out, the floggings with the knout..." Svetlana covered her mouth and shook her head from side to side. "You have to do what she says. Yes you do."

Colonel Tchichagov placed his right ankle across his left knee and nodded. "I am glad to see that someone in this house understands the way royal protocol works. I was beginning to wonder if your father had neglected his duty of instructing his daughter in the ways of the world." Again, he made a point of inspecting her from head to toe.

"My father abandoned nothing." Alyona could think of no other reply, but her mind was spinning, searching for some clever response. Something to put Tchichagov in his place.

"I am glad to hear that. Then you understand that you must begin to pack, because we will leave by the end of next month. You are to remain here through the Lenten season but must arrive at the Winter Palace in time to accompany the entourage to Tsarskoe Selo. There you will fully participate in the summer season, as was your father's original plan for last year."

A summer of frivolity and parties sounded so wonderful. Yet, being absent for such a long time would almost guarantee that the estate would be lost. "Smallpox was not part of my father's plan, however. I am needed here in order to continue the smooth running of my household."

He shook his head. "The empress has already thought of these things. She has made arrangements for the purchase of your home so this will not be a burden to you. The income from that sale will act as a dowry."

"A dowry?"

"An orphan is not particularly prized as an advantageous

match in St. Petersburg society, especially one whose father gave up his title and inheritance to marry a street urchin. You will need some sort of bait to lure in potential suitors." He quirked his left eyebrow. "Thankfully you are pretty enough that some men might be willing to overlook your obvious lack of breeding —" he sighed then, long and loud, "assuming a very large sum is part of the deal."

"How dare you."

"How dare I what? Speak the truth? You are nothing but a commodity to be traded at court." He stood. "You have three weeks." He nodded toward her, then waited for Svetlana to lead him through the doorway.

Alyona resisted the urge to strike him as he strutted past. How dare that pompous buffoon insult her mother! Her life had been far more valuable than a dozen of his, regardless of the fact that she was born with no rank or connections.

She walked over to her father's desk and ran her fingers across the fine scrollwork around the edges, her mind flying in a million directions. What was she to do?

Svetlana hurried back into the room, accompanied by Cook. "Is it true, then?"

"Apparently so." Alyona looked at Cook, who had been the voice of wisdom in her life since the death of her mother three years ago, and nothing short of a parent since the death of her father a year and a half ago. "What am I to do?"

"It would seem there is not much choice in what you will do. The choice is elsewhere."

"What do you mean?"

"Remember what your mother always taught us. 'Focus on God's blessings, the things that you have, and not the things that are out of your control.'"

"I feel as though I am losing everything I had left."

Cook shook her head. "There are things that remain. Tell me what they are."

"I cannot see any."

"I will say, I will. You get to live at court." Svetlana clasped her hands together under her chin and drew up her shoulders with excitement. "Beautiful balls, handsome men." She twirled around, then curtsied. "A summer in Tsarskoe Selo is what you have always dreamed of, it is, and now you get to do it under the direct care of the empress."

It was true that all of her life she had yearned for this. Only not this way. Not without her parents. Not at the cost of her home and all the people who worked in it—the closest thing to family that remained.

"She is correct." Cook nodded. "And I have been watching you run yourself ragged trying to keep everything together here for far too long." She put her finger under Alyona's chin and lifted her face so she looked her in the eye. "We both know that it is a failing venture."

The reality in these words stabbed her. As hard as she had tried, she did not possess the ability to keep it all going. Everyone could see that, including her. She dropped her head. "You are right."

"Do not hang your head, child. You have done more than any woman twice your age could have done. You leave us here, in the hands of the empress, and this place will survive to honor your father's legacy. You go on to court and find the destiny you were meant for. Remember your mother's words. 'Sometimes storms and shipwrecks are needed to get us where we are supposed to go.'"

"Just think. Your shipwreck is landing you right in the middle of a palace. Just think, just think." Svetlana bounced up and down. "That is the best kind of wreck, don't you agree?"

CHAPTER 4

"The sale of the estate has been finalized." Alyona handed Cook the letter.

"It is for the best, child."

"Is it?" Relief that she was no longer tasked with a burden too heavy to bear, mingled with excitement at her imminent new life at court, mingled with grief at leaving everyone she knew and loved behind—especially Cook. After leaving here, Alyona would be a true orphan.

As most of the household servants had worked here since she was born, they seemed more like family in many ways— other than the boundaries of propriety her father had insisted they keep. Still, she had to admit, Svetlana could be quite clingy and overwhelming. It might be nice to have a maid who was a little less...suffocating.

On her morning walk, Alyona determined to focus on her blessings. She began counting the steps of the waltz—one, two, three, one, two, three. In her mind she saw the young man— wavy dark hair, flashing brown eyes that gazed upon her with admiration. He bowed and asked for the next dance, then took her hand and began twirling. And twirling. And laughing.

She stared into his eyes, which had now changed to blue, and heard him saying that she must not dance with anyone but him for the rest of the evening. She fanned herself and batted her eyes, as she had heard the sophisticated ladies at court often did. Only when she'd twirled herself dizzy did she start back toward the house.

As she entered the back door, sobs emanated from the pantry area. The kitchen itself stood empty, which was unusual this time of morning. She walked toward the sound, soon recognizing that the wheeze-sniffle-snort pattern could belong to only one person. She hurried forward. "Svetlana?"

"Shh." The crying quieted marginally as Cook came through the pantry door and closed it behind her. "Good morning, mistress. It's nice to see you up and about. Shall I serve your breakfast in the dining room?" She walked toward Alyona as she said this, effectively pushing her farther away from the pantry.

"Why is Svetlana crying?"

"Do not concern yourself with that."

Alyona made to move past her. "Svetlana?"

Cook grabbed her by the arm and turned her around. "There's no reason to go in there, mistress. Nothing can be done. Your pity will only make matters worse."

"Pity for what?"

"It does not concern you."

Alyona jerked her arm free. "Pity for what?"

Cook lifted her apron to wipe at the corner of her left eye. A trickle of tears moved down her right cheek, which she also dabbed. "Do you know much of Colonel Tchichagov's son?"

"Nothing whatsoever. I know only the colonel, whom Father always declared to be the most pretentious and worthless man who has ever drawn breath."

Cook nodded grimly. "His son is far worse, as he is not only pompous but also known for his debauchery. Every serving girl in the city knows to avoid him."

"What has that got to do with Svetlana?"

"She caught his eye a couple of years ago. He made repeated offers to your father to purchase her. The general always refused —never bothering to mention that she was not a serf and he didn't own her. Now, the son has gone to his father, who is friends with the new overseer—whoever that mysterious person may be. It has been arranged for Svetlana to be released from service here and sent to work at the son's estate."

"But she is free. She does not have to go."

"Who do you think will hire her? No one wants to be on the colonel's bad side, and anything that displeases his son displeases him. Since he is the highest-ranking official in town, it would not be in anyone's interest to offend him. This leaves her with one choice. Starve to death, or go to the son's estate."

"That is not fair."

"It is the way things work."

"Not while there is breath in my body."

Alyona stormed from the room and up the stairs, having no idea what she was going to do, but knowing she had to find some way to save Svetlana.

CHAPTER 5

$\mathcal{D}$ay after day, Alyona sent out pleas for a safe placement for Svetlana. Rejection after rejection answered, until her hopes shriveled and died. Cook had been correct. No one wanted to risk angering the colonel, especially not for the sake of some orphaned servant girl.

Svetlana refused to speak of it. She carried on, dry-eyed, shoulders back, and her voice silent for the first time in her entire life. The quiet hung heavy across the entire house.

On the morning Alyona was to depart for her new life, Svetlana was also to depart for hers. Alyona's many trunks were packed and stacked near the front door, Svetlana's one trunk was placed out back. It was the first time in her life that Alyona felt truly powerless. She finally understood what it was like not to be backed by a strong champion like her father.

Three wagons, laden with furniture and trunks, pulled up the circular drive in front of the house. Alyona went out to greet them. "I believe you must have the wrong address. We were to be sent an empty wagon to convey my trunks to St. Petersburg."

The driver removed his cap in respect. "Yes, mistress that is what we are to do. First though, we are to unload the colonel's belongings into the house. Then we will put your trunks into the wagon."

"The colonel's belongings?"

"He is the new resident, mistress."

The colonel? Now things were starting to make sense. Of course Colonel Tchichagov would want to take over one of the finest homes in the city. One that had been owned by the general, no less. How dare he? Fury boiled inside Alyona at yet another thing over which she had no control.

She marched up the steps to the front door and stood there, blocking its entry. This she could do. At least for now. "You'll not bring even a stick of that vile man's things into this house. Not while I'm still here."

The drivers of all three wagons looked at each other as if to decide what to do with this crazy lady. Finally, the man from the first wagon looked at his comrades and shrugged. "As you like, madame."

For the next hour, the men loitered near their wagons. They unloaded everything to the ground but made no attempt to carry anything inside. Alyona brought out coffee, bread, and cheese, which the men accepted, but she couldn't help but notice how they kept glancing nervously toward the gate, waiting for their master to appear.

Over an hour later, Colonel Tchichagov's carriage arrived. Alyona marched out to meet him, waiting only until the door opened before she said, "What is the meaning of this?"

He stared down his long, crooked nose at her. "The meaning of what?"

"Your things being brought into my home?"

"It is no longer your home and has not been for two weeks now. You have been living here on my good charity."

"*Your* good charity? I sold this estate to the empress."

He shrugged. "And the empress rewards those who serve her well." He gestured toward the house. "When I explained to her that it is in such wretched condition but that I would be willing to take the burden off her by paying for the upkeep required, she was happy to sell this house to me."

"This house has been maintained impeccably." Alyona thought of the meticulous care her father had taken to make certain of this. In fact, there was likely not another home in all of the Russias so well-tended.

"That, of course, is the opinion of a young girl who knows nothing of such things."

"I know that yours are the words of a greedy conniver who lies whenever he speaks."

He waved his hand in a dismissive gesture. "Again, your opinion. I care nothing for it." He strode into the house and barked orders as to the placement of furniture.

The empress rewards those who serve her well.

The words spun through Alyona's mind until they landed in one clear and beautiful idea. She spoke to the carriage driver. "There is one more trunk that was left behind the house. Could you please fetch it and load it for me?"

He doffed his cap. "Of course, mistress."

She frantically ran through the house until she found Svetlana and grabbed her by the arm. "Come with me. Quick."

Sometime later, the colonel emerged from the building. "I am to accompany you on the journey. The passage is not safe, and it would not do to lose you before the empress decides to send you away herself." He opened the door to the carriage, then stopped. "What are you doing in here? Get out at once. The wagons will convey you to my son's estate."

Alyona came right up behind him. "She is coming with me."

"I bought this house. Therefore, I own all the serfs who are part of it. She stays."

"My father owned no serfs, as you very well know. Each and every servant in his employ were just that—in his employ."

"Her employment has been terminated already, due to the fact that her work is reported as not being up to standard."

"She has been terminated from the household staff, yes, but she is currently in my employ as my own personal maid. She will be accompanying me to court."

His eyes narrowed. "You do not have authorization to do that."

"The empress rewards those who serve her well, you said so yourself. I think we both know that my father served the empress very well, and I am more than certain she would want his bereaved daughter to have her personal maid who has been with her since she was a small child."

He glared at her but seemed to know that he would not win this battle. Finally, he flipped his hand toward the driver's seat. "I'll not ride in a carriage with a servant. She can sit up top."

"And I'll not ride in a carriage with a buffoon. *You* may sit up top." Alyona had never in her life spoken in such a way to another person, let alone an adult, and a man, but she had taken all she could take.

His mouth dropped open. Quickly enough, he closed it and drew himself up to his full height. "As it is a fine day, I shall ride my horse for the first leg of the journey. However, we will eventually encounter bad weather. At that time, she must make other arrangements." He turned on his heel and stomped away.

"We will see about that," Alyona called after him before she climbed into the carriage and took her seat.

Svetlana leaned toward her, tears brimming in her eyes. "Oh, mistress. Thank you, thank you."

Alyona clasped Svetlana's hand. "You can count on me to do my best to take care of you. Always."

Svetlana sniffled, then looked out the window, where the Colonel was now pacing back and forth on a black horse. "I cannot believe that such an awful man will be in charge of the household. Oh, what will the others do? He may not be like his son, but he's mean, just the same."

Alyona was more than certain she was correct about that. "I wish there was something I could do to help them. All of them." She looked at Svetlana, who was leaning toward the window for one last glance as they pulled away. "Let me know what you hear, won't you? I doubt that Cook would write to me with complete honesty, but she will tell you. I'm not sure what I can do for them, but I need to know the truth so I can try."

"I will tell you. I promise."

The carriage pulled away from the house, and they said no more for a long time. Alyona was thankful for this, as Svetlana tended to chatter on endlessly. She looked over and saw the girl had tears streaming down her cheeks, had apparently done so for quite a while as wet patches stained the front of her sarafan. Alyona reached out and squeezed her shoulder. "It will be all right."

Svetlana wiped her face and nodded. "I know." She offered a wobbly smile. "Cook reminded me this morning of your mother's old saying. Remember? 'Storms and shipwrecks...' She said your father's death didn't catch God by surprise like it did the rest of us. And as much as me being in this carriage on my way to St. Petersburg right now surprised me—and the colonel even more—God knew."

The memory of her mother's voice cut through her. How many things her mother believed and held tight to. Still, those things sounded better in theory rather than applied to one's own life. She nodded toward Svetlana and choked out the words, "Cook is a wise woman."

"She learned from your mother."

Alyona's mother had seen to the education of her entire household. She found it appalling that even many nobles in Russia were illiterate, and vowed that no one in her home would be denied the chance to learn, regardless of their status. She also demonstrated the way to live with generosity and kindness. Svetlana's very presence was a testament to that.

Her father had been killed in an accident during the harvest several years ago. Alyona's mother took food and comfort to his widow, who was herself in poor health. It was she who begged Alyona's mother to take Svetlana on as a servant.

Svetlana was the youngest of the brood by almost a decade. The rest of her siblings were married with children of their own to feed and could not take on the extra burden. Alyona's mother had agreed, and Svetlana had been with them ever since. While not raised as an equal to Alyona, she was still treated with regard and dignity. Svetlana's mother died soon after, and only now did Alyona realize how little she had understood the pain of being an orphan—until she became one. "I am thankful that we have each other for this journey and what's beyond."

"So am I, mistress, so am I. Thank you for not leaving me behind."

"You may depend upon me. I will keep you safe." As the carriage made its way through the city, Alyona prayed she could keep that promise.

CHAPTER 6

May 1752
St. Petersburg, Russia

As the days passed, Alyona made sure Colonel Tchichagov came to understand that if he was going to ride in the carriage at all, he would indeed share it with a servant. One particularly cold morning, he climbed aboard, making a great show of his loud sighing. "While we may ride in the same space, I shall not deign to speak with the creature."

Alyona offered an accommodating smile. "Of course, you would feel that way. I am sorry for your discomfort and shall ease you as best I can." She leaned toward him and whispered, "I do not speak to anyone who feels that speaking to my friend is beneath him. Therefore, I believe you may expect to continue the next two weeks without ever feeling the burden of engaging in conversation."

Svetlana giggled at this and then the carriage went quiet. For the next couple of days, conversation happened only between

Alyona and Svetlana, or more truthfully, Svetlana, chatted endlessly and Alyona listened. The colonel sighed so often, Alyona finally said, "Perhaps you would prefer to ride your horse for this segment of the journey?"

His face grew bright red, but he said nothing. The sighing decreased after that but did not cease.

At last, they pulled up to the main entrance of the Winter Palace. Constructed of stone with an imposing sloped roof towering over four stories of windows, it overwhelmed the gardens, trees, and other fine houses nearby. Svetlana gasped. "Have you ever seen anything so grand?"

Colonel Tchichagov waved his hand dismissively. "This old ramshackle thing? *Pfff.* Anna Ivanovna did not have the exacting taste of our current empress, who already has Monsieur Rastrelli, an Italian architect, perfecting plans to completely rebuild this old, drafty thing. This will truly be a marvel when it is finished. Something worthy of our motherland."

"A marvel," Svetlana whispered and looked at Alyona, eyes wide.

"Wait here. I shall let them know of our arrival." The colonel exited the carriage.

"Can you believe we are here?" Svetlana said it again. "Soon enough there will be balls, and parties, and feasts. Just like we've always dreamed." Her face was close enough to the window that the glass began to fog up. "Look at those foot-men. Their uniforms are every bit as fine as your father's. Who could imagine such a thing, a footman dressed as well as a general?"

The colonel opened the door. "They are ready for us." He extended a hand. "Mademoiselle Balashova, allow me."

"Unless you plan to extend your hand to Svetlana as well, you may go elsewhere."

"I most certainly will not. It would be beneath me."

"Then we will both make our own way out." She would not

have Svetlana's first memory in their new home as one of being snubbed.

"It would be considered inappropriate for me to allow you to climb out without my assistance."

Alyona looked toward the dozens and dozens of windows. Who might be watching that made him so nervous?

"Then assist Svetlana first."

Whoever he suspected of watching apparently vexed him enough that he extended his hand. "Hurry up, then."

"Why, thank you, sir." She took his hand and spoke in her most polished voice. He jerked his hand away from her the second her feet hit the ground, and he reached up to assist Alyona.

"Your gallantry is most appreciated," she said.

A maid wearing a black wool dress made her way out to them and curtsied. "I bring you Her Majesty's special greetings, Mademoiselle Balashova. Please allow me to show you to your chambers, where it is requested that you freshen up quickly. Her Imperial Majesty is eager to see you and will receive you in one hour."

"Her Imperial Majesty will receive us?" Svetlana's hand went to her throat. "I cannot believe this."

"Of course she won't receive *you*, idiot. She was speaking of Alyona Arkadyevna, the daughter of the general." Colonel Tchichagov's tone carried a note of fear. So, he had not expected this.

Svetlana's face turned bright red. "Of course not me. I knew that."

The maid stood watching all this with great interest. Alyona suspected that the story of this exchange would spread throughout the servants' quarters before the sun set. Svetlana would be humiliated.

"How dare you, sir? Whether or not this young lady has a title to make her eligible to be presented to the empress, you have seen her noble character over these past weeks of travel. She has done nothing worthy of anything but the highest respect. For a man who calls himself a gentleman to use a word like *idiot* to describe such a young lady calls your very own nobleness of character into question, does it not? A question also posed by your dealings with my father's estate. Perhaps the empress should be made aware of this questionability."

At these words, it was the colonel's turn for a red face. "I apologize. I meant no offense."

She continued to stare at him. "It was not me to whom the wrong was done, nor is it I to whom the apology is owed."

He glared at her in a challenge, but she held his gaze. Finally, he looked toward Svetlana. "Apologies, mademoiselle."

Svetlana bowed her head graciously. "Accepted." She turned to Alyona then. "Shall we go to our chamber? We've got to prepare you to meet the empress." She let out a little squeal with this pronouncement, which garnered another annoyed look from the colonel, but he didn't dare say anything.

"Follow me, please." The maid walked quickly up the stairs and through the door. They made their way through winding corridors and up a narrow set of steps. "Your room, for now at least, will be on the hall with the maids of honor." She glanced toward Svetlana. "You will be in the maids' quarters."

"Of course," Svetlana said in her most dignified voice.

They walked a long, quiet corridor until they stopped at the last room on the left. It contained a bed, a nightstand, a chest of drawers, and a large wardrobe. "Your trunks will be brought up momentarily. In the meantime—" the maid raised her hand and signaled Svetlana to follow— "I will show you to your room."

"I cannot go now. I need to help my mistress get ready."

"You can return here after, but we are all very busy. I need to show you now."

"But I—"

Alyona reached out and squeezed her arm. "Go. I am certain you can be back in plenty of time to assist me."

Svetlana departed, looking back nervously over her shoulder as she did. Alyona walked around the room, unable to quite believe she was really going to live in the palace. Within moments, the footman arrived with her trunks. "Should I send one of the maids up to help you unpack?"

"No, thank you. I can take it from here."

"Very well." He disappeared down the hall.

As predicted, Svetlana was back in just a few minutes. The excitement in her eyes had been replaced by...what? Disappointment? She busied herself emptying the trunks without uttering a single word.

"Is all well?"

Svetlana didn't answer at first. Finally, she looked up, her right eyebrow quirked high. "I have a bed with the royal maids. Who would believe that back home?" Still, her subdued manner led Alyona to understand that the royal maids' quarters were less glamorous than she had hoped.

"This dress is lovely, but it's a shame you will not be wearing your velvet ball gown when you meet Her Imperial Majesty."

Alyona laughed, but it was more from nerves than humor. "Somehow I don't think showing up in a ball gown in the middle of the day would give the empress confidence in my suitability to be presented at court."

"It's just like you've always dreamed. A beautiful dress. The royal court."

"Yes." Neither of them stated the obvious, that the dream had not included the death of her parents.

Svetlana was pinning up a braid when a couple of beautiful young women came to the door. They appeared to be Alyona's age and were dressed in sumptuous gowns, which made Alyona feel a bit shabbily attired. The first, a tall, elegant girl with white satin ribbons woven through her black braids said, "My name is

Belka, and this is Sabina. We are maids of honor to Her Imperial Majesty and have been sent to escort you to her antechamber."

"Thank you so much. I am certain I could never find my way by myself. The corridors are all so very confusing."

Sabina snickered. "Do not worry about it. You will not be here long. Her Majesty tends to marry off girls for whom she has no use."

Girls for whom she has no use?

Belka narrowed her eyes. "Sabina, that sounded unkind, although I am certain you did not intend for it to be so."

Sabina's eyes grew wide. "Oh, did it? I apologize. It was not intended that way at all. Please forgive me."

"Of course." Alyona gave a single nod.

"It is only that we've had what…three weddings already this month? Every time the empress shows her magnanimity by sending for the orphan of someone of lesser birth…" She held her breath for a moment, making a show of stifling a giggle.

Belka shot her a warning glance, then turned her attention to Alyona. "The empress does love to attend weddings. She often arranges marriages as rewards for her guards." She paused for a moment. "Or punishment for courtiers who have displeased her."

Sabina chimed in. "She comes dressed as a peasant to some of these arranged weddings. She owns thousands of beautiful gowns and refuses to wear the same one twice, but for commoner weddings she likes to relax and enjoy herself. She dances and dances and dances. It's one of her great joys."

"You are making a joke." Svetlana regarded the girls, brows knitted in doubt.

Sabina rolled her eyes and then turned back to Alyona. "Some people who do not understand the royal ways would never believe this, I suppose. But those of us in the inner circles know that this is just part of it. The empress can do what she wants, when she wants, regardless of whether other people…"

She stopped long enough to glare at Svetlana. "Especially serfs —" she paused again for effect "—find it eccentric or unbelievable."

Svetlana's ears had gone red, she was so embarrassed. Alyona looked at Sabina and spoke in a quiet, and she hoped polite, voice. "Svetlana is not a serf. She is my friend."

Sabina lifted her chin and peered down her nose at Svetlana. "My *friends*—" another pause long enough to let the venom of the word sink in "—do not spend their days darning socks and washing clothes."

"Then perhaps you have chosen the wrong kind of friends.'

Belka looked at Sabina and gave an almost-imperceptible shake of her head. "We had better hurry. You know how Her Majesty feels about being kept waiting."

They made their way out of the room, and just like that, Alyona found herself following two haughty girls, toward the woman who controlled her fate.

CHAPTER 7

*E*mpress Elizabeth sat in the middle of the room, wearing a splendid dress of deep purple silk embroidered with pale-pink thread. Semiprecious stones, sewn all around the neckline, glistened beneath ropes of pearls draped around her neck. A dozen or more courtiers lined the room, each scrutinizing this newcomer with interest.

Alyona moved forward when prompted and curtsied.

"So. You are the daughter of the bravest of all generals, Arkady Alexandrovich Balashov."

"Yes, Your Imperial Majesty." Alyona could see that the legendary beauty of the Russian empress had not been overstated. In spite of being in her forties, the woman's creamy skin did not have a single crease, and her blue eyes were every bit as piercing as was often repeated throughout the territories.

"Your father's passing was a great loss to our Mother Russia."

Alyona wasn't certain whether she was expected to agree with the empress or remain silent. She took a breath, noting how the entire room had gone quiet, perhaps waiting to see what she might do. Were they all watching for her to make a mistake? What would even be a mistake in this case?

Finally, the empress spoke again. "What is your name, girl?"

"Alyona Arkadyevna Balashova."

The empress nodded slowly and said nothing for far too long for the silence to remain comfortable. Finally, she said, "Come closer, Alyona Arkadyevna Balashova."

Alyona moved closer to the large red velvet chair with gilded arms.

Even here, in the empress's private chambers, there could be no doubt as to who ruled this land. "Turn."

"Your Majesty?"

The empress made a circling motion with a couple of fingers. "Turn."

Alyona turned around, feeling silly. She glanced back at the empress, still unsure if she had done what was being requested of her.

"Slower. Turn slower." The empress spoke with a breathy voice, almost purring. The sound of it made Alyona feel as though something were crawling up her spine. Something cold and ominous.

"Yes, you are lovely, just as your father always told me."

Papochka had discussed her with the empress? Alyona could not have been more stunned. Still, she remembered her courtesy. "Thank you, Your Majesty."

"You have been shown to your room? Found it adequate? Is there anything you require?"

"My room is wonderful and I have all that I need, I thank you."

"Good. Good. You may go and rest from your journey now." She nodded toward one of the maids of honor, a girl perhaps a couple of years older than Alyona, with plump cheeks and shiny black hair pulled back in a simple twist. "Vanya, see to it that she is outfitted for Friday."

"Of course." Vanya curtsied, then gestured for Alyona to follow her.

Once outside the antechamber, she said, "My name is Vanya. Please feel free to ask questions of me. It can be a little intimidating here, especially with no parents to offer guidance. I am certain that must be difficult for you."

No parents to offer guidance. The truth of the words knocked the air from her lungs. "Thank you. I would be glad for the help. I know absolutely nothing about court life."

"Let us start with the basics, shall we? I will show you where the small dining room is. Supper is at eight." Her round face and dark eyes had a serene expression that Alyona found comforting.

"I shall never figure it all out."

"That is just as well, you will not be here long."

"Will I not?" Somehow the words hurt more coming from someone who had seemed so kind at first.

"We will all be leaving for Tsarskoe Selo—Tsar's Village—in a couple of weeks. We spend the summer there, at the Catherine Palace. By the time we get back here for the winter, renovations will be underway. The court will be scattered elsewhere while Monsieur Rastrelli guts these interiors. So you see, there really is no reason to be terribly concerned about learning this place. Just the basics will do."

A beautiful palace to be gutted? What extravagance! *"Overspending, overeating, overdressed peacocks."* That's what her father had always said about life at court and the people who chose it. The remembrance of those words stabbed at the edge of her conscience, but she set the thought aside. Everything was going to be fabulous. Completely glamorous.

"Let's walk down to the royal wardrobe and see if we can sort you out something to wear to Friday night's ball."

"Friday night is a ball?" Alyona's voice cracked with excitement, but she didn't care and couldn't have helped it if she did.

Ball gowns… If only she had kept the fabric the empress had sent before her father's death. Had she been hasty in selling it? No. What else could she have done? They needed the money to keep the household running. At least she had kept the one gown that had been complete the day her father was to have arrived. "I brought a velvet ball gown with me. As it is still cool at night, I believe it might be appropriate."

Vanya laughed. "It most definitely will not be."

"I believe you should look at the dress before you rush to such a judgment." Alyona allowed anger to infuse her voice. She was tired of this double talk from the women here.

Vanya stopped walking and turned, putting her hand to her throat. "Oh no, please. You misunderstood my meaning." She shook her head. "I am certain that your dress is lovely and look forward to seeing it in the future. It's just that this Friday is a metamorphosis ball."

"A metamorphosis ball?"

"Yes. All the men have to dress like women—petticoats and panniers and all—and the women have to dress like men."

"You are joking."

"No, but most men of the court wish that I were."

"I must believe that they do." Alyona thought about what her father would have said about going to a ball dressed as a woman. Actually, she knew exactly what he would have said. *No.*

"The empress has very shapely legs, you see, and wearing a closely fitted guard's uniform enables her to show them off quite nicely." Vanya grinned. "She makes no secret of this motivation."

Alyona considered the apparel she'd packed in her trunks. Including her father's uniform. She had brought it to keep him close in memory, but what if she had his uniform altered and wore it? It would be keeping him close all the more.

"Perhaps a trip to the wardrobe will not be necessary. I actually brought my father's uniform with me. Would something like that be appropriate?"

"It would be perfect. However, wasn't your father a large man?" Vanya stopped and looked at Alyona. "You are tall, for sure, but I doubt your small frame would fill your father's jacket. The empress does not like for garments to be sloppy."

In truth, her father was a large, barrel-chested man with a ruddy complexion. Alyona had her mother's fine bones, thin build, and pale skin, but she was taller than most other young ladies. She had to find a way to make it work. "I brought along my maid who is a wonder with sewing. I am certain she can alter it suitably."

Vanya nodded. "In such case, I think it would be marvelous. It will be an honor to your father's memory."

"Yes." Alyona was thankful that for her first royal ball, she could not only pretend to be someone else, but that someone else would be her father. She would somehow gain from his strength.

CHAPTER 8

"*I*t's just wrong, that's what it is. Wrong. Wrong. Wrong." Svetlana made *tsking* sounds as she circled Alyona. "I already wrote Cook to tell her all about it. I can hardly wait to hear what she has to say."

"Knowing Cook, it will be something thoughtful and deep."

"Likely." Svetlana tilted her head to the side and nodded her agreement, but soon a smile emerged. "But Ilya will have something a little shallower and funnier, and that's what I most look forward to hearing. Yes, I do."

Alyona laughed at this. "I have to admit, I look forward to hearing Ilya's take on the whole thing, too." Cook's husband, Ilya, was her opposite in almost every way. Somehow, they were perfect together. Yes, his comments on this masquerade would be worth reading, just as Cook's deeper words would be something to hold on to. If only she were here now.

"Well, if I can't make you the most beautiful courtier there, I'll at least make you the most handsome." Svetlana pinned a braid across Alyona's head. "You know how your father used to call the women at court overdressed peacocks? Well, wouldn't he just roll over in his grave if he knew you were going to your first ball dressed as him?" Both girls exploded into fits of laughter.

Belka entered the bedchamber, wearing a splendid evening coat of burgundy silk and gold brocade, a ruffled shirt, along with britches and riding boots. Sabina followed in a similar ensemble, but hers was an emerald green. She gasped when she saw Alyona. "I did not believe it when you told me your father's uniform would be ready by tonight, but I have been proven wrong."

"Yes, Svetlana's skill with a needle and thread has proven many people wrong." Alyona could sense Svetlana tense behind her, waiting for a caustic reply.

Belka moved in for a closer inspection, running her gloved fingers around the seams of the coat. "The girl does have a fair amount of skill."

"The *girl* has a name. She is Svetlana, and she has more than a fair amount of skill."

Sabina folded her arms across her chest. "Let me give you some advice. You clearly do not belong here—as evidenced by your low birth and your choice of friends. Perhaps you should spend this evening focused on finding a man and winning his favor before the empress chooses for you. You never know how that will turn out."

Belka looked toward Sabina with a grin. "Usually not the way you'd like."

They both giggled. Belka said, "Come. It is time to depart. We must be in the grand ballroom to greet the guests when they arrive." The two of them made their way out into the hall without waiting to see if Alyona followed.

Svetlana approached close behind her and whispered, "Ignore those two cows. It is your first royal ball. Enjoy every magical moment, just as you've always dreamed. Find yourself a handsome prince and dance the night away."

Alyona turned and grasped her hand, noticing that her own had a slight tremor. "Thank you, Svetlana."

Svetlana cocked her head to the side. "Although, I have to say I question the judgment of any man who would want to dance with someone who looks like your father."

Alyona held her breath as she walked from the bedchamber, careful to keep the laugh inside. But oh, she was thankful for it.

THE GRAND BALLROOM WAS BEYOND ANYTHING Alyona had ever imagined. Thousands of candles flickered from crystal chandeliers beneath ceilings filled with painted frescoes and gilded trim. On the wall, large sconces flanked by gilded mirrors made the entire room appear to be filled with dancing candlelight. The polished wood floor boasted the design of many large ovals of intricately woven flowers and vines created from the interspersion of dark and light wood. It was a shame this would all be torn down soon. Alyona hoped they salvaged these beautiful furnishings and used them again.

She looked up from her reverie to notice that the entire room was staring at her. Of course, Belka and Sabina were among Elizabeth's closest maids of honor, but Alyona suspected more of these stares were curiosity checking out the newcomer. A small crowd was assembled now—the maids of honor, the gentlemen of the court, all here early to make sure the guests were properly greeted.

"When will Her Imperial Majesty arrive?"

"Soon. Her predecessor always arrived very late at these events, letting everyone know that she was too important to be bothered. Empress Elizabeth, however, loves to dance. She will be along in time to lead the opening waltz."

A servant came forward with a tray of champagne, vodka, and brandy. Both of the others took the brandy; Alyona opted for the champagne. She took a sip and the bubbles made her sneeze. The two women laughed. "You have much to learn."

"Such as how to drink this without sneezing?"

"Such as Her Majesty likes cherry brandy. So, therefore, you learn to like cherry brandy."

"Or at least pretend you like the foul stuff when you are at an event where she'll be in attendance." Belka took a sip and then screwed up her face. "Blah."

A tall man with broad shoulders and a dimpled chin, wearing a hoop skirt, a fully rouged face, and a wig of blond hair, made his way over to them. "Good evening, ladies. Or should I say, gentlemen? And who, might I ask, is this new soldier who has joined our ranks this evening?" He made a pretense of batting his eyes and fanning himself.

"May I present Alyona Arkadyevna Balashova. Alyona, meet Prince Andrei Dmitritovich Naryshkin." The blush that spread across Sabina's cheeks told Alyona what she already suspected— Prince Naryshkin was very handsome in his regular state of dress.

Remaining in character as a woman, the prince curtsied. Alyona followed the cue and bowed. "Balashova? You must be General Balashov's daughter? That explains the fine uniform."

Alyona nodded and gazed down at the glass in her hand, suddenly thankful for its presence. It gave her something to focus on rather than how awkward she felt. Prince Naryshkin moved closer. "Where are all the medals?"

"It would not be right for me to wear them. They were earned by my father."

"Yes, but you are dressed as your father tonight."

"I may be dressed in his uniform so I can pretend to be a man, but I do not believe that it would be appropriate to pretend to be brave and fearless and honorable. Those are the kinds of things that must be earned, not pretended."

"Well said." He lifted his own champagne glass up in a toast, and they all clinked glasses.

Sabina moved a step closer to him. "Tell us, Prince, will you be spending the summer in Tsarskoe Selo this year?"

He glanced at Alyona before answering. "I had planned to go to Moscow to spend some time with my father. But I may reconsider. There is time to decide later. What do you think, Mademoiselle Balashova? Where should I spend my summer?"

The question was a test, but to what end? "I think only you can determine the answer to that question, but my thought is to spend it among people you cherish most."

"People I cherish most, hm?" He offered a lopsided grin, his bright-blue eyes twinkling. "I will have to think about that."

Just then, the empress entered the grand ballroom on the arm of a young man, dressed in a gown of pale-yellow brocade. He held his chin quite high, and although Alyona had no idea who he might be, she understood without a doubt that this man knew that he wielded much power.

The empress herself was dressed in the uniform of the Preobrazhensky Guards and wore a man's wig. Her pants were closely fitted to her legs, which were quite long and shapely, just as Vanya had said. The empress nodded toward the orchestra leader who lifted his baton in the air.

Prince Naryshkin extended his hand toward Alyona. "Will you dance with me so we might continue the discussion of the summer and cherished people?"

"I would be honored." She took his hand and, as she passed her champagne to Belka to hold, did not miss the look of annoyance on Belka's and Sabina's faces. This made her somehow happy, although Cook would not approve of such churlish thoughts.

They opened with a waltz. Alyona was thankful for that, as

the waltz was her most practiced dance. Soon she lost herself in the beauty of the music and the room. If only her father were here to experience all this with her.

"You seem to have floated to another place. Have I grown boring so soon?" Prince Naryshkin tilted his head to the side, studying her closely.

She felt herself blush. "I do apologize. I was thinking of my father."

"Oh, I am sorry. You must miss him very much."

"I do, but I wasn't thinking about him in that way just then."

"What then?"

"I was wondering how he would feel to know that I attended my very first ball dressed in his uniform. I am sure he would have much to say about it, and most of it quite amusing."

"Your first ball? And I am your first dance partner at your first ball?"

Had she really just admitted that? Alyona wished the ground would open up and swallow her.

The prince twirled her around. "You have done me a great honor. Perhaps the greatest of my life."

Alyona's cheeks grew hot. "I think you overstate this, sir."

"I would beg to differ, but as my face is covered with rouge, I suspect it will be hard for you to take me seriously, regardless of what I might profess."

Alyona laughed outright. "That is perhaps correct."

"Then we will just have to make certain that we see each other soon, under less...contrived circumstances? Should we not?"

"Perhaps." She hoped she sounded sufficiently coy. In truth, she wondered about his normal appearance. All she could determine for now was his dimpled chin and quirky little grin. She could not deny that she hoped to see more of both in the future.

As the waltz ended, they made their way toward the side of

the room. "I shall deposit you with your friends for now, but please save the mazurka for me."

"I would be honored." How she wished she were dressed as a woman so she had a fan. It was entirely too warm in here.

When they came to where the others were still standing, he bowed toward Alyona, then looked toward Sabina and Belka. "I think summer in Tsarskoe Selo is sounding more likely all the time." He sank into a mock curtsy, then walked away.

CHAPTER 9

The next day, the maids of honor gathered in the small dining room, groaning about headaches and exhaustion as they drank tea from brass samovars and coffee from gleaming silver pots. Alyona, who had barely slept, felt perfectly wonderful.

"You look perky for someone who danced every single dance last night." Belka's face was even paler than usual, giving the impression she might be sick at any moment.

"I must admit, I feel quite well." Alyona sighed.

"You enjoyed it then, even though your many suitors wore corsets?"

"That did make it a bit less romantic, I must confess. But still, it was thrilling." Alyona toyed with her water goblet, wondering yet again what Prince Naryshkin looked like in normal life.

"Of course you would think so. Every man there was fighting for a chance to dance with you," Vanya said without malice. "Which was difficult since Prince Naryshkin seemed to be there for more than his fair share." This brought several glares her way, but Alyona did not care.

Sabina rubbed her forehead between her thumb and middle finger. "It's a good thing Princess Maria wasn't there. She would have been furious."

"Who is Princess Maria?"

"Prince Naryshkin's fiancée."

"His very jealous fiancée." Belka stirred jam into her tea but made no attempt to take a sip.

"What?" Alyona's stomach churned. "He is engaged? He most certainly didn't seem—"

"He never does."

"Are you saying he's a scoundrel?" At this point, all-out laughter erupted from the two girls.

"We are saying he is a man."

"Does he not love her?"

"He loves her family's lofty position at the royal court. And their fine estate near Moscow."

Hot tears threatened to spill forth. Alyona blinked hard. "Are all the men at court like this?"

Vanya leaned forward and looked at Alyona with something like pity in her eyes. "You really are upset, aren't you?" She reached out and petted Alyona's hand. "Might as well get used to it. That's just how it works."

The last time she'd heard such words, they were spoken by Cook about Svetlana being handed off for a lifetime of abuse.

"If that is true, I want nothing to do with the way things work." Alyona thought of her father. He was gruff, in fact many people would describe him as offensive, but no one would ever say that he did not cherish his wife with all his heart.

"The empress was watching you last night," Vanya said.

"More likely she was watching her legs." This comment came from one of the maids of honor whose name Alyona could not remember. She continued, "When she sees another set of shapely legs show up at court, that woman usually gets sent away pretty quickly."

"Especially now that the empress is getting older and rounder." More giggles burst out.

Why did everyone keep telling her how quickly she was going to be sent away? Alyona was tired of it and determined that she would prove them all wrong.

She pitied the empress. These women were supposed to be her closest confidants, yet they showed her no true loyalty. She was someone they could use to get where they wanted to be. Another example of "just the way things are," which made her all the more thankful for Svetlana. Even if she was no more than a servant in the world's eyes, she was worth more than these glamorous fakes—even if she did talk and talk until Alyona's ears ached.

As they finished eating, a messenger arrived for her. "The empress would like to see you in her chambers after lunch."

Alyona stood and made her way through the dining room. She could hear whispers behind her. "I told you she wouldn't last long."

THE EMPRESS WAS RESPLENDENT IN A GOWN OF mustard-colored silk. A tray of what appeared to be candied fruit sat on the table beside her, and she picked up a large red piece and popped it in her mouth as Alyona approached. Although her entire body trembled, Alyona curtsied and forced a demure smile. Necessity required her to stay alert and ingratiating to avoid any stray word or action that could find her married off and sent away.

"Good afternoon, Alyona Arkadyevna," she spoke as she chewed.

"Good afternoon, Your Imperial Majesty."

She stretched out her left arm and motioned Alyona toward her. "Please, come closer. Let me take a look at you now that you are once again a woman."

Alyona stepped closer and the empress touched the sleeve of her dress. It was a pale-blue silk, simply adorned but with lovely gold cording around the bodice and waist. "Your father employed a skilled seamstress. I am thankful to know that he did not raise you as a complete barbarian."

Alyona could have told her that the skilled seamstress of which she spoke was a teenage orphan currently living in the maids' quarters in this very palace. Somehow, she knew instinctively that this piece of information would have Svetlana removed from her service and into the empress's before she left this chamber.

"Your father was a brave man. Mother Russia owes him much. And yet, he was not the most charming of men to speak with, was he?" The empress picked up another piece of the candied fruit and examined the sugared surface of an orange sphere before she placed it back into the bowl. "You are an elegant dancer. I am assuming that you attended many balls in Kazan?"

"No, Your Imperial Majesty. Last night was my first."

"Last night was your first ball?"

"Yes, Your Majesty."

She reached back into the bowl, pulled out something yellow, and popped it in her mouth. "But you dance so well."

"Thank you, Majesty. My tutors taught me. My father and I were to have attended the winter season in Moscow upon his return from surveying the Volga settlements." The weight of the words pressed against her chest. "Of course, that was one and a half years ago. His death changed everything."

"Such a sad situation." The empress made a clucking sound and drummed her fingers on the arm of the chair. Her fingernails were perfect ovals, oiled to a light pink. "Tell me, how did you enjoy your first ball?"

How should she answer this question? This was the empress of all the Russias, not a confidant with whom she might be completely honest. "It was beautiful."

"And did you enjoy the attention of all the young men? I saw that you got more than your fair share."

"I believe all the young ladies were also receiving plenty of attention, but I have to confess that I did enjoy it. I have heard some rumors this morning, however, that make me believe that not all of the young men were pure in their intentions."

The empress raised a manicured finger to tap her cheek. "You might have trouble finding a young man at court who meets those expectations." She looked toward one of her ladies, then tilted her head toward Alyona. "What about Captain Balabanov? He is a man of integrity, is he not?"

Alarm bells began to clang within Alyona's head. She did not want to be married off because she seemed ungrateful. She offered what she hoped was her most precocious smile. "I may have difficulty finding a young man of pure intentions, but I certainly look forward to the search, Your Imperial Majesty."

The empress laughed. "Good for you." She nodded. "Yes, we shall see that you have plenty more opportunities." She picked up another piece of fruit and popped it in her mouth. "Many more indeed."

"Thank you, Majesty." Was she supposed to leave? Perhaps she needed to wait until she was dismissed, so Alyona stood there, hands clasped at her waist, and waited.

The empress studied her for a long time, as if trying to make up her mind. "I do believe that you make a fine addition to court. Perhaps the Grand Duke Peter's entourage might suit you better, as the group is young and gay. Unfortunately, they have already departed for their summer in Oranienbaum. In the meantime, you shall accompany us to Tsarskoe Selo, where you will continue to live among my maids of honor. You will be allotted a salary for clothes, and all your other needs will be provided."

"It will be an honor to serve you, Your Imperial Majesty." Again Alyona curtsied, almost falling over with relief not to have been married off on her first week at court.

"ARE WE BEING SENT AWAY?" SVETLANA GRABBED Alyona, pinning both her arms, and squeezed hard. "Please do not leave me, do not leave me please."

With effort, Alyona pried her arms free and smiled into the frightened girl's face. "No, we are not being sent away."

Svetlana collapsed into the chair. "Thank goodness. That's what they were all saying, that the empress would marry you off to some horrible old noble and you would be packed away to his estate and I would be left out on the streets."

Alyona knelt beside her, took her hands, and kissed them. "Dear Svetlana, you have been the truest of true to me. I will not let them turn you out, I promise you."

"How can you promise? The empress can do whatever she wants."

"Yes, that seems to be true. However, I would never do anything that involved leaving you out on the streets. Even if we have to run away and leave the country altogether, we would somehow make it work."

The fear in her eyes finally lessened. "Why did the empress summon you?"

"I am to become a maid of honor in Grand Duke Peter's court."

"A maid of honor? Really?" Svetlana sighed with happiness.

"Yes, but we will not go there right away. We are to spend the summer in Tsarskoe Selo with the empress. The younger members of the court spend their summer in Oranienbaum and are already there. We will join them when they return to St. Petersburg for the winter."

"They all gossip about his wife, the Grand Duchess Catherine. She was a princess from some insignificant place, and the empress brought her here to marry the grand duke. They say he doesn't like Catherine very much, and if she doesn't produce an heir soon, things will not go so well for her. Her husband already has a full-time mistress."

"How awful. And how awful it must be to have so many eyes upon you when your life is already hard."

"All those jewels, and dresses, and all that fine food. I could put up with a mean husband for half of what she's got. Yes, yes."

"Perhaps." Alyona nodded, but she thought about what she'd learned. "I look forward to meeting her at the end of the summer. Perhaps she needs a friend."

Later that night, Alyona lay in bed with visions of befriending Grand Duchess Catherine. She pictured the two of them walking into ballrooms together, laughing and sharing confidences, just two friends who did not care for the backbiters at court.

She fell into a deep sleep, her dreams full of hope.

CHAPTER 10

The Catherine Palace in Tsarskoe Selo was much more grandiose than the Winter Palace. The building itself was the color of the sky, with columns and trim painted pure white, and an excess of gilded cupolas. Alyona longed to see Svetlana's face at this moment, to hear the gushing appraisal she was most certainly bestowing upon the occupants of the servants' wagon.

"It is amazing." Alyona turned to Vanya, who sat beside her in the carriage.

"Yes. Peter the Great built it for his wife, Catherine—Empress Elizabeth's mother. At the time it was nothing special, but Her Imperial Majesty is making the effort to turn all the royal residences into something more appropriate for her station."

"Like the Winter Palace will be?"

"Exactly. Soon, it will exceed even this palace in its splendor. The empress will see to it. It is important that all the courts of Europe understand that Russia is their equal. She wants every one of her palaces to rival Versailles. The French have always been convinced they are the sole possessors of fine court life."

As they were helped down by a finely dressed footman, Vanya took her by the arm. "Allow me to show you around. After the empress arrives tomorrow, it will be difficult to access some of the rooms, and there is one in particular that you simply must see."

They made their way through ballrooms, staterooms, dining rooms, and a large gallery, before they entered the room that took Alyona's breath away. "I can't believe it." She turned in a circle, looking all around, having no clear idea of what to focus on first.

Vanya laughed. "I am not surprised."

"What is it?"

"Amber. Almost the entire room is made from it—except, of course, for the gold, mirrors, and paintings."

"It is truly the most beautiful room I have ever seen."

"I told you this, did I not?"

Alyona paused at each intricately carved panel made of amber mosaic. The sheen was so rich and deep, the beauty of it actually brought tears to her eyes. There were carvings of amber, sculptures in relief formed from amber, surrounded by frames of different shades of amber. Mirrors encased in frames of amber added depth and light. What an honor it was to be able to live among such beauty. It was even more than she had dreamed about as a child.

Her hands lifted of their own accord, but she knew these treasures were not to be touched. No matter how great the temptation. Inch by inch, she made her way around the room, transported to a place of joy she'd never known. Such beauty. Such amazing beauty.

"Shall I show you to your chamber now?" Vanya's voice drew her back to reality.

"I am sorry. I was so lost in the perfection of this place, I quite forgot that you were standing there waiting for me."

Vanya smiled. "I am pleased to see that you appreciate it for the wonder that it is."

Alyona vowed that she would bring Svetlana back to this room this very evening. She could hardly wait to see her reaction.

As they entered the hallway for the maids of honor, half-a-dozen footmen bustled about, carrying large trunks, their faces red with exertion.

Vanya paused outside the second door on the right. "I have arranged it so your room will be next to mine. I hope that is acceptable to you."

"Acceptable? I am so grateful."

Vanya gestured inside. "Do not be surprised if some of the others are upset by this. The rooms are usually arranged in order of rank, so by rights, you should be at the far end of the hall. However, since you are not to stay with us past the summer's end, I made the decision to arrange you in a more convenient location. And to be honest, it was a selfish act on my part. I find you more agreeable than many of the current maids of honor. They are mostly backbiting intriguers."

"I am glad to have your friendship."

Vanya looked at her thoughtfully, then nodded. "Friendship. Yes."

Just then, Belka and Sabina made their way past, glowering at Alyona. Varya smiled sweetly at them. "A mail delivery has arrived. There will be readers in the library for the rest of the evening for your convenience."

Readers? It had never occurred to Alyona that these glamorous ladies of the court could speak French and put on all sorts of airs but could not read or write. The education, or lack thereof, seemed so contradictory. She also offered a sweet smile. "Or, if that is not convenient for you, I would be happy to read your letters for you." Alyona lifted an eyebrow in the way she often saw Belka do. "Or if you prefer, my maid Svetlana could do so, as well." She regretted the words the minute she spoke them. That kind of pretention was beneath her.

They walked away and she looked toward Vanya. "I apologize for that. I do not know what came over me."

"The two of them can lead all of us to behave in ways that would not be our normal. Do not reproach yourself any longer." Vanya gestured inside. "Your maid and your trunks have arrived."

Alyona entered the room, which surprised her, in both size and elegance. The pale-blue walls had gilded insets around gilded sconces, and a lovely Russian stove, covered in white and blue hand-painted tile, stood along the back wall. She noted the small writing desk with several letters sitting atop it and her heart swelled. Letters from home. What a perfect day. Svetlana, busy at her task of unpacking, did not turn toward them or even acknowledge their entrance. Strange.

"Much nicer than your old room, yes?" Vanya traced her fingers along the gilded frame of a small mirror. "The recent renovation here gives you a glimpse of what shall become of the Winter Palace over the next few years."

Alyona twirled around, unable to believe that she was actually going to be allowed to live in such a wonderful place. "This is amazing."

Vanya smiled. "I shall leave you to get settled."

No sooner had Vanya walked away than Svetlana rushed over and grasped Alyona's hands, her face streaked with tears. "I've had a letter from Cook. That colonel, he is a bad man."

Something sharp and icy poured through Alyona's veins. "What has he done?"

"First, he cut the wages of the entire staff by half. When some began to complain, he fired them all."

"All? Impossible. It takes many people to run that household."

"He brought in serfs from his other estate."

"Serfs?" The word took the breath from Alyona. She sank onto the bed. "My mother would never have allowed serfs to work in that house."

"No, she would not. Nor would she have cut her servants' pay in half."

"Has anyone been able to find work?" Alyona stood and began pacing. "What can we do to help them?"

"Thankfully your father's friend Monsieur Linkov has hired a few. Some of them live on their own small farms so they will be able to survive until something else comes along—*if* something else comes along."

And that was the problem. There were few owners of estates who were seeking hired labor. It was more efficient and much less expensive to simply own serfs. Alyona shook her head. "Mother must be rolling over in her grave right now."

"Likely. The colonel did offer Cook her regular wage to stay on."

Alyona laughed bitterly. "I am not surprised. It is rare to find anyone who cooks as well as she."

"True. She has refused, though. She said that she would not work in the house of a man who behaved in such a way."

"Good for Cook." Alyona's heart thumped with pride.

"Except the colonel is very angry. He is making it hard for all of them."

"None of this would be happening if I were still there."

"The household would have been lost either way, though perhaps more slowly if you had remained. That is all." Svetlana pulled out another gown, shook it with a snap, and laid it atop the bed. "Here is where you must be. There's nothing you can do for those left behind, besides pray for them."

"And that I shall do." Alyona looked toward the trunks. "Let's remove the icons now and set up our prayer corner, shall we?"

"Yes."

They quickly did so, but it gave Alyona little relief. Praying felt too much like doing nothing, and right now, she had to do *something*. She just didn't know what.

CHAPTER 11

"There has never been a ball gown as lovely as this. I am certain of it." Alyona positioned her tortoise shell mirror in a variety of angles, trying to see as much as possible. Before they left St. Petersburg, she had spent every bit of her dress allowance on thick Russian silk, enough for several dresses. Svetlana had transformed each into a work of true beauty.

This weekend's celebration was to include two balls as well as general feasting and merriment. Alyona thought she might burst with the thrill of it all.

The gown was white, and Svetlana had trimmed it with gold embroidery. "It is understated. Yet so elegant."

Svetlana nodded. "I agree with you that it is very beautiful, but I do worry about the understated part. I hope the other ladies in their really fancy dresses don't make you feel uncomfortable. I know my work isn't as intricate as theirs."

"Uncomfortable? In this?" Alyona fanned out the skirt on both sides. "I couldn't possibly."

"It's a shame that your original ball gown is not appropriate. It is so much fancier."

"And it will be lovely this fall, when the air is colder. I am more than certain that heavy velvet in a packed ballroom in the summer would be enough to make me pass out."

"I suppose you are right. It was made for the cold, and it will be perfect in a few more months."

Alyona made her way to the dressing room at the end of the hallway and studied herself in the long mirror. Everything about this dress was perfect, from the cone-shaped top to the pannier that was less wide than many at court but still wide enough to be stylish. She went back to the room and hugged Svetlana. "It is so incredible." She twirled around, watching the fabric swish around her. "I wish that you could come with me."

Svetlana made a dismissive gesture. "Me? With all those fancy people? I think not. But..." She flounced up a ruffle at Alyona's shoulder. "When you return you must tell me everything. Lots of details, yes, yes."

"Indeed I will."

They hugged one last time and then Alyona walked into the hallway to join the other maids of honor as they paraded to the ballroom. Tonight was going to be the night she'd always dreamed of. She just knew it.

THE GRAND BALLROOM WAS NOT SO DIFFERENT FROM the one at the Winter Palace. Gleaming chandeliers, thousands of flickering candles, mirrors, and gold-leaf trim. Seeing women dressed like women and, more importantly, men dressed as men made this one so much more romantic, though.

Prince Naryshkin arrived early and immediately made his way toward her. Seeing him now, dressed as a man, his wavy blond hair and bright blue eyes so very compelling, she took a deep breath. She steeled herself, determined not to fall victim to his false charms.

"My dearest Alyona." He picked up her gloved hand and kissed it. "I should have known that as well as you looked in a general's uniform, you would be simply stunning in a ball gown. Still, you take me by surprise. Might I request the honor of the first dance?"

Everything inside of Alyona wanted to just accept the offer for what it was, but she would not allow herself to do so. "And what of Princess Maria? Will she not want the first dance?"

"I am certain she agrees that we need to ensure the newest members of court feel welcomed here."

"I am certain she will understand better that her fiancé should offer the first dance to no one other than herself."

"My fiancée?" The prince looked truly surprised. "You have obviously been listening to idle chatter. I would have thought you above all that."

"Are you saying that you are not betrothed?"

"Precisely."

Alyona studied his face, uncertain what to believe. "I...but they all said—"

"Princess Maria's mother and my mother have been lifelong friends. There has always been speculation of a betrothal, but it is nothing more than that, idle speculation." His eyes twinkled in the candlelight. "Never have I been more thankful to be unattached than I am at this very moment."

"Then I would be most honored to take the first dance with you. I apologize for allowing myself to believe that you were anything other than honorable, Prince Naryshkin."

"You must call me Andrei." He bent down to kiss her hand one last time. "I thank you for the honor. Now, I must go and speak with some of my father's friends—dispense with the obligatory niceties—so I may enjoy the rest of the evening with the most beautiful girl in the ballroom." He bowed again and walked away.

Alyona's face burned with...what? Embarrassment? Pride? Could it be love? She thought it might be a combination of all those things.

He wasn't betrothed! He wanted to spend the evening dancing with her. He called her the most beautiful girl in the ballroom. Everything she had hoped for, it was all coming true.

CHAPTER 12

*B*y the third dance—all three with Prince Naryshkin...
Andrei—Alyona was growing more convinced that
this might be what love felt like. He was so funny, and charming, and handsome. She could not believe she had been chosen
—the lucky girl who had gained his attention. She tried not to
take anything for granted, but there were a lot of other girls, all
beautiful, all dressed more opulently than she. And he had
chosen her.

"Shall we walk outside? It is getting warm in here, and the
evening is so lovely." He extended his elbow, and she placed her
hand in the crook of his arm.

As they walked through the crowd, she could feel the
envious stares from the other girls. She didn't look at any of
them but kept her eyes straight ahead.

"My family has an estate not far from here. Would you do me
the honor of a visit? Perhaps someday soon I could send the
carriage for you and we could spend the day exploring the
grounds. I believe you would like them. In fact, I'm hoping that
you feel right at home there."

Right at home. Alyona's head was spinning. It was all too impossibly wonderful to be believed.

They strolled through the open double doors and saw the empress standing out on the balcony. She was speaking with an elegantly dressed man, who looked familiar, although Alyona could not place him.

"Even the empress knows that it is much too beautiful a night to spend all her time indoors. As much as she loves to dance, you know the night must be spectacular, indeed."

And it was. This time of year it never grew fully dark, but the twilight sky was so full of stars, they seemed to be piled on top of each other, each trying to outshine the one beside it. "It is so incredible." She sighed and shook her head at the beauty of it.

"You are incredible." He led her to a tall hedge, effectively separating them from palace view. "So very incredible," he whispered the words as he leaned forward and brought his lips to hers.

So this was what love felt like! He drew her close, and she wanted to stay like this forever. When his arms loosened behind her, she held on all the tighter. She could not bear the thought of letting him go.

His hands pressed against her waist, then slid up her ribs, and to the top of her bodice. For a moment she froze, stunned by this blatant action. Soon, however, her brain awoke, and she pushed back and slapped him. Hard. "What do you think you are doing?"

He released her and stepped back, placing his hand on his cheek. "Do not be like that. I would have thought you above playing coquettish games."

"I play no games, sir. You seem to have mistaken me for a tramp." She gathered her skirt and rushed toward the side of the hedge, back toward the party and people and safety.

He grabbed her by the arm, his face softened. "Please, I am

sorry. Truly I am. It's just that you look so lovely, I quite lost track of myself." He tilted his head and studied her, his cheek red where she had slapped him. He offered a repentant grin. "You have wounded me heart and soul, mademoiselle, and I beg your forgiveness. I have often been told my ego could use a bit of taking down. On behalf of all mankind who will appreciate the newer, more contrite version of me, I thank you." He extended his elbow. "Allow me another chance to behave like the gentleman I strive to be."

He sounded so sincere, and she so badly wanted to believe him. But how could she?

The sound of music wafted from the ballroom, and laughter, and dancing feet. Only moments ago, those sounds held so much promise. Now...maybe it had all been an illusion. The events of the last few minutes confused her greatly. No gentleman would behave in such a way...would he?

"Please, I pledge that I shall behave with the utmost decorum. It would be scandalous if we were seen returning and I was not escorting you properly. People would talk, and you would carry the brunt."

Knowing this was true, she did reach out and take his arm, but it made her stomach churn. As they approached the palace, for the sake of prying eyes she tried to appear calm and serene, although she did not feel that way.

The empress still stood on the balcony with the same man. Everything about him put off a puffed-up-because-I'm-so-handsome air. The empress, however, didn't seem to mind this, and she tapped him on the shoulder with her fan and lowered her head to laugh, flashing him a flirtatious smile.

"Who is that man with the empress? He seems familiar to me somehow, but I can't think of how I would know him."

Andrei stopped walking and took her chin in his hand, pulling her gaze up to meet his. "Already thinking of my replacement?"

Her mouth had gone so dry, all she could manage was a whisper. "Should I not be?"

He looked deep into her eyes. "I will do what it takes to earn your forgiveness. Believe me, I can be a very determined man."

She felt herself acquiescing. She wanted to forgive him. She wanted all to be well. But she did not want to be a fool. "You have a long journey ahead."

Andrei smiled at that. "I gladly accept the challenge." He glanced up toward the balcony. "Oh, that is Vadim Tchichagov."

"Colonel Tchichagov's son?"

"Yes. You know him?"

"The colonel purchased my home in Kazan. I do not know Vadim, but I do not believe he is an honorable man."

Andrei coughed. "There are few people who do believe that. None, I would venture, unless he considers himself so."

They returned to the ballroom and joined a waltz already in progress. Alyona couldn't help but notice Andrei scanned the crowd as they danced, something he had not done before.

At the end of the song, he bowed toward her. "If you will excuse me for a moment. I see someone I need to speak with." He kissed her hand and walked away.

As Alyona watched him go, she longed for the comfort of her mother's voice. Or the sound advice of Cook. This was all so much more confusing than she had expected.

"Might I be so bold as to ask for the next dance?" Startled by the voice behind her, she turned to see Vadim Tchichagov very near to her.

She glared at the awful man. "I am not inclined to dance at this moment."

Only then did Alyona notice the empress at his side, scowling. She fluttered a swan-skin fan toward her face. "What is this I hear? Surely you have not refused my dear friend the honor of a dance?"

"I...uh..."

"Alyona Arkadyevna, I simply must see you dance with Vadim."

Alyona did not want to touch the foul man, but as the empress demanded it, she had no choice. "Yes, I thank you, sir."

She followed him out onto the dance floor. He pulled her in a little closer than necessary and whispered, "Our little Alyona has grown up." He spun her around, then pulled her back in close. "Father told me as much, but I had no idea."

The room around them seemed to cease activity, with all eyes focused directly at them. Watching him. He was handsome to a fault, but it was not necessary to even speak with him to see his arrogance, and she knew he possessed far worse qualities. She looked forward to granting the other women in the room their wishes of dancing with this peacock. She, however, wanted away from him and quickly. Hopefully Andrei would rescue her as soon as the song ended, although it seemed to drag on forever.

Vadim whispered in her ear, "The empress is watching you quite closely tonight."

The feel of his breath on her neck gave her the urge to run away, but she would not give him the satisfaction. "You are mistaken, sir. The empress takes no more note of me than any other insignificant person in this palace."

"You are correct in saying she does not notice people of no significance. That is, unless it is either a handsome man or a woman who is so beautiful she feels threatened. I fall into the first category, and I believe you have fallen into the second."

"Your assertions are erroneous." She stared him straight in the eye. "On both counts."

He scoffed. "Well, well, well. My father said you were a shrew. Now I know of what he speaks. Still, I always did like a good challenge."

The orchestra played their final notes, and as they bowed to each other, she said, "I suggest you exert your efforts elsewhere.

They are wasted here." Alyona hurried back over to stand with Vanya. "That man is foul."

"Be careful what you say. There are many ears here."

"What does that matter? I am speaking truth."

"Speaking that sort of truth, about someone who has the favor of the empress, can land you in a place you do not want to be."

Prickly needles crept up Alyona's spine. She knew she had much to learn, but she did not want to think about such things. She scanned the room and saw Andrei standing amidst a group of people, talking and laughing. As it would be inappropriate for her to go to him, she stood in place. He would seek her out soon.

"Your Imperial Majesty." Vanya bowed, as did Alyona, when the empress approached.

"Why are the two of you not dancing? I refuse to have my maids of honor being dull during a party." The empress turned to a servant at her side. "Go and fetch Colonel Yakov and Count Vorontsov and tell them they must come dance with my ladies immediately."

The servant bowed and made his way toward a group of men assembled around a card table at the back of the ballroom. Alyona had noticed the group earlier, well-dressed men who called greetings to most everyone but seemed a bit too smug to mingle with the assembled mass. Lots of loud laughter and plenty of vodka flowing.

Soon, two men appeared. The first seemed to be acquainted with Vanya. They exchanged greetings and then made their way to the dance floor. The empress took the elbow of the remaining man. His face was handsome, with high cheekbones and a mischievous twinkle in his eyes, which she guessed had seen close to forty years. He also wore a long beard. This fact alone told Alyona that he was of some standing in the royal court. Beards had been outlawed during the reign of the empress's father, Peter the Great. Now, men were forced to either be clean shaven or pay a beard tax. Still, in the great palaces, there were few around. "Lev Petrovich, I simply cannot bear watching General Balashov's daughter standing idle for one second longer. Please escort her to the dance floor."

He bowed. "It would be an honor, Your Majesty." He extended his elbow to Alyona and led her into the waltz with skill.

His green silk jacket was trimmed in a gold brocade, which gave a fine appearance but not overly pretentious like Vadim Tchichagov's. "I knew your father. He was a true patriot."

"Thank you, sir. He did his best to serve his country."

"You are new to court, yes? Are you finding it to your liking?"

"Of course it is all beautiful, but I'm afraid there is much for me to learn."

He spun her around. "Please feel free to call upon me if you find you need assistance of any kind."

The offer sounded sincere, and for the first time since her arrival, Alyona thought she might have met someone who had no ulterior motives other than to be kind. "I thank you, sir."

He smiled. "The empress has forced you to dance with me, instead of the younger, handsomer sort, so let's see if I can at least entertain. Which would you prefer to hear about? The time a rat crawled into Countess Platova's wig—while she was wearing it—or the stable boy who took the empress's sleigh for a joyride and broke through the ice of the Neva, narrowly avoiding losing her favorite team of horses as well as the sleigh?"

Alyona laughed. "I would like to hear both, actually."

"Aha. I have found an attentive audience." For the rest of the dance, Count Vorontsov regaled her with funny stories. None of them were mean-spirited, but all of them made the other members of court seem a little less intimidating, a little more human. When the final note played, he bowed. "I thank you for the pleasure of your company." It seemed as though he truly meant it.

THE GRAND BALLROOM WAS STIFLING, AND ALYONA considered stepping out onto the balcony to cool off. She chose not to because she wanted Andrei to be able to find her. They needed to talk more tonight, to settle things. He would understand this and come to her soon.

She took a goblet from one of the passing servers and sipped, hoping for relief from the heat. Instead she felt the burn of cherry brandy down her throat. It led her to a fit of coughing, which she stifled as best she could, but not before tears were streaming down her face from the exertion.

"May I have this dance?" A young man she did not recognize extended his hand. She let him lead her to the dance floor, as she discreetly dabbed at her eyes.

The young man introduced himself, and she did the same. He was older than she but much closer to her in age than Count Vorontsov. She tried to show polite attention to her partner, as she surreptitiously scanned the room for Andrei. She did not see him, but Alyona did notice Count Vorontsov watching her. He nodded a greeting, then turned back to his card game.

When the song ended, she could not remember the name of her partner. She was thankful that he did not stay around to chat afterwards because it saved her the embarrassment.

Vanya came up to her. "We should walk outside."

"I...well..." Alyona did not want to go outside. She wanted to wait here.

"It is necessary." Vanya took her by the arm and led her

toward the door— the same one she'd gone through with Andrei just a few hours ago.

It did feel refreshing to breathe in the cooler outdoor air. Air not weighed down by perfume and sweat. She inhaled deeply. "This is nice, thank you, but I don't want to stay out here long."

"You must."

"But why?"

"You are garnering far too much attention."

Alyona held up her fan and shook it toward her face. "No more than—"

"Listen to me," Vanya almost hissed. "This is no time to be coy. You are getting a lot of attention, and that does not fail to draw the attention of the empress. Believe me when I tell you, you do not want to rouse her jealousy."

"But she is the one who told me to go dance."

"Yes, with partners she chose, correct?"

"Yes, but I do not understand the problem."

"Let's hope that you never have to. I am just telling you that for now, you need to get out of her sight."

They walked to the balustrade that overlooked the courtyard. Couples strolled near the pond, where the stars reflected back in twinkling agreement with how wonderful this night was. Alyona looked toward the hedge and saw another couple emerge, both straightening themselves and laughing. Arm in arm, they moved closer, until their identity became perfectly clear.

Andrei and Sabina.

A wave of nausea nearly overcame her, but Alyona managed to fight through it with measured breathing.

Sabina glanced up to where Alyona stood, leaned even closer to Andrei, then waved up to her. There could be no mistaking the look of victory in her eyes.

CHAPTER 13

*T*ables laden with exotic fruits, caviar, imported cheese, and smoked venison were spread outside on this absolutely perfect day. The sun shone upon intricate paths of stone, shrubs, and well-tended flowers. Conversations floated through the air, declaring the complete success of last night's ball, Sabina's voice loudest of all. Lots of "It was so romantic," and "I cannot remember a more beautiful night," being punctuated by dramatic sighs.

"You look downcast this fine day. I find that hard to believe given the rousing success of your first true ball." Vanya stirred a spoonful of jam into her tea, all the while studying Alyona.

"Was it a success? Before my parents died, I dreamed of coming to court and living amongst all the splendor. I believed that I would find true love and happiness here, just as they found in a more drab life. I wanted both, you see."

"Your parents then, it was a love match?"

"Oh yes." Alyona sighed. "It was quite the romantic story. Scandalous, too, for that matter."

Vanya rested her chin on her hand and leaned forward. "Do tell. I simply must hear it."

"My mother, you see, was a shopkeeper's daughter. Her father had taught her to read and write at a young age, and she was skilled at bookkeeping. Beautiful by all accounts, but her manners were..." Alyona pondered for a moment how to tell this story truthfully without sounding as if she was speaking ill of her mother. "Less refined."

"Less refined?"

"She was not crude, but she liked to laugh as much and as loud as any man in the room. She used to say, 'Women spend too much time pretending to be less intelligent and less fun than they really are.'"

Vanya laughed. "There is plenty of truth in that."

"Yes, I agree. So did my father, apparently. He was from a noble family near Moscow. In spite of the fact that his parents had tried to arrange a suitable match for him, he wanted nothing to do with marriage.

"One Christmas Eve, on his way to his family's estate, he heard the sounds of shouting and soon saw the reason why. A runaway troika came careening toward him. It was obvious that the driver had lost the reins and the horses were out of control. He blocked the path with his own troika. The runaway horses turned into an embankment, thus ejecting my mother and sending her flying headfirst into the snow.

"My father jumped down and ran to her. She was lying face down in the snow, and he feared she was dead or badly broken. He turned her over and could see that she was bleeding. Just then she coughed, spit some bloody snow out of her mouth, coughed again, and said, 'The horses? Are they all right?'

"My father couldn't believe it. He said, 'What about you?' She spit out a little more blood and replied, 'I'm perfectly fine as you can well see. Now, what about my horses?' He said, 'They too are perfectly fine. More so than you appear to be.' She nodded, then said, 'Do you have a gun, sir?' My father could not understand the question and asked for what purpose. 'To shoot the impudent beasts.'"

Vanya laughed. "It does sound as though your mother had her own will."

"Yes, she did." Alyona pictured her face, although the clarity of it was beginning to fade from memory. "My father said he knew right then, as mother sat in the snow with blood streaming from her nose and a nasty bruise already forming on her cheek, that this was the woman he had waited for all his life. He asked to see her safely back home, and she considered herself insulted, saying she had two more visits yet. She was doing the traditional late-night Christmas Eve visitation, you see. He asked if he might accompany her on the next visits.

"Mamochka was once again insulted that he thought she required his assistance, until he said, 'I can see that you are quite capable. It's just that from your eagerness to visit these neighbors, I can only assume they are much more pleasant than my own family. I should dearly love the excuse to delay my arrival for a few more hours.' She looked up at him to glare, then seeing the entreaty on his face, she burst out laughing, as did he. She said she knew by the end of the first visitation that she could love none other than him. At the end of the night, he did at least follow her back to her home. Within the week he had asked for her hand in marriage."

"Oh, how romantic. Were they married during the Yule season, then?"

"Oh no. She refused him for some time."

"Refused him. Did you not just say that she loved him?"

"Yes, with all her heart. His family, you see, had several large estates with thousands of serfs. My mother declared that she would not be married to someone who thought that owning another human being could ever be acceptable."

"How did he finally persuade her?"

"He renounced his position as heir. His father was livid and cut him off completely, bequeathing everything to a distant cousin. As a final jab, his wedding gift to my father was the estate in Kazan and all the serfs who worked on it. He believed that my father would have to choose between owning the serfs or selling them along with the estate.

"Instead, he gave all the serfs their freedom and offered to pay them what wages he was able. That estate grew quite profitable, so they were well compensated. My father said that a free man working for his own wage would be much more productive than a prisoner with no reason to do more than the bare minimum."

"Is that how you got your maid who is with you, too?"

"No. She was born to a free man. Her father died in an accident and her mother had long been ill. She asked my mother to take Svetlana as a servant in the great hall. She wanted her to have an education and to be safe. My mother did both."

"Your mother educated your servants?" Vanya sounded truly scandalized. "I thought you were jesting when you offered your maid to help read Sabina's letters."

"Not a jest. I spoke the truth." Alyona looked at her evenly, proud of her mother. Proud of the shocked response this almost always elicited.

"It sounds as though you came from a remarkable family." Vanya glanced toward Sabina who was whispering and giggling. "Make certain that you do not allow manipulative people to change you, no matter how hard they try."

CHAPTER 14

"*I* have been thinking about you all day. Will you do me the honor of the first dance?" Prince Andrei, impeccable in his white silk jacket with red sash and gold epaulets, placed his right hand over his heart in flirtatious supplication.

"I most certainly will not." Alyona glared at him. "How could you even ask me that after the way you behaved last night?"

He moved closer and lowered his voice. "I am begging your forgiveness. I am much ashamed, though you are partly to blame."

"*I* am to blame?"

"I saw you dancing with Ivan Golubov, you see." He picked up her gloved hand and kissed it. "I am ashamed to admit that it put such a surge of jealousy through me that I lost control. I wanted you to feel as awful as I did in that moment. It was beneath me. Although I do not deserve your forgiveness, I ask for it once again." He smiled his little lopsided smile. "You, it seems, bring out both the best and the worst in me. Please dance with me tonight so I might renew your faith in me."

He looked at her with such innocence shining from his blue eyes. Still, he had proven himself to be untrustworthy, how could she believe him?

Just then, she noticed Sabina watching them from across the room, mouth set in a hard line. Alyona knew that if she refused Andrei, Sabina would be waiting. So, she fanned herself and batted her eyes in a flirtatious way, or at least she hoped that's how it appeared. "One more chance." Whether this was for his benefit or Sabina's, she could not say.

"I shall cherish the opportunity." He led her onto the dance floor. Once again, her stomach did little flip-flops at his attention, but this time she knew better. She could not trust him, no matter how her heart yearned to.

After the third dance, Andrei led her from the floor. He whispered into her ear, "Would I offend you if I asked you to take another outdoor stroll?"

She took a step back, reeling as if she'd been struck. "You mistake me, sir. I am not stupid."

He sighed dramatically. "This is a problem I have brought upon myself. I shall make it my duty to change your mind before the evening is over."

"I wish you luck, but I think you might sooner hear lobsters singing on the mountains."

"Then I shall move closer and closer in the anticipation of hearing their song." He stepped toward her, flashing the lopsided grin.

"There you are." Vanya pushed herself between the two of them and turned to Alyona. "Could I have a word with you please, in private?"

Alyona opened her eyes wide, trying to signal her friend that this was not a good time. "Of course, but can it wait until later?"

"I am afraid that it cannot. I—"

"There you are." An absolutely breathtaking woman came to

stand between Vanya and Andrei. Her dress, a pale pink satin trimmed with pearls, and her perfectly curled blonde hair, framed a cherubic visage. Alyona knew by instinct that this woman was beloved by all who knew her.

She shot an impish grin toward Andrei. "I've been searching for you for some time. Have you been hiding from me?"

Andrei laughed with seeming delight. "How can I be hiding from someone whom I was not expecting until next week? You returned from Moscow early."

Vanya also smiled at the woman, but it did not seem genuine. "Princess Maria, may I present Alyona Balashova. Alyona, Princess Maria Sokolova."

The two women curtsied toward each other, then Princess Maria installed her hand in the crook of Andrei's arm. "Should I be jealous to find that my fiancé has met this newest member of court before I?"

Her fiancé? Alyona looked toward Andrei, waiting for him to assure them all that Princess Maria was jesting. Waiting for him to say something, anything, that would remove the dagger currently twisting in Alyona's heart.

Instead, he smiled so warmly, so genuinely, toward the princess. "You are the one who asked me to be more social, are you not?"

"Yes, but I said that about my father and his card games, not about the tasty morsels that attach themselves to the court. Tell me you have not been placing wagers with your friends again about how many women you could lure behind the hedges."

The ballroom started to spin. Somewhere, as if from a great distance, she heard Andrei's voice. "Of course not, dearest. I was fortunate enough to meet Mademoiselle Balashova while we were still at the Winter Palace. You had just departed for Moscow."

"Oh yes. Mother and I went early..." The conversation continued, but Alyona heard only the buzzing in her ears. He was betrothed? Wagered with his friends about how many women he could lure behind the hedges? Was there no end to his treachery?

She thought up an excuse of someone she needed to speak to and ran out of the ballroom, planning to shut herself in her room. Permanently. Someone grabbed her arm and jerked her around.

"Count Vorontsov, I must go—"

His face, devoid of its usual carefree openness, was drawn and serious. "Get control of yourself. You cannot leave. Every tongue in the palace would be wagging by morning."

"I do not care." She pulled her arm out of his grasp.

"You will care plenty by the time tomorrow dawns, this I can promise you. Those women in there—they look for signs of weakness in someone like you. Once they find it..." He shook his head. "You must keep your head held high. Do not let them win." He extended his elbow. "Come, let's dance. There are many eyes upon you. You must prove that you are above all the pettiness."

"I cannot."

"You can, and I will help you." He continued to hold out his arm until she took it and followed him onto the dance floor.

After a few minutes, she regained enough of her thoughts to realize what Count Vorontsov had just done for her. "I thank you for your kindness, sir."

He dipped his head. "You have much to learn about life at court. When I noticed Naryshkin casting his eye toward you, I knew there was trouble ahead. I am sad for your sake but thankful, too. I believe you escaped relatively unscathed."

"Unscathed?" That did not feel true, but in reality, she had to admit that it was. "I suppose so. I just do not understand."

"Your heart is too pure for all this hypocrisy. Take my advice and get away from the court as soon as you are able. Before you, too, fall prey to its treachery."

"But the empress, she is so devout. I am told she performs penance on the chapel's stone floors on swollen knees for hours at a time. Why does she allow her court to behave in such a way?"

Count Vorontsov shook his head. "There is much pretense that goes on in these hallways. Piety is at the top of that list." He stayed with her through several songs, until she had regained her composure, then nodded toward Vanya at the edge of the dance floor. "I see your friend looking for you. I shall take my leave now." He bowed toward her and walked away.

Alyona somehow made it through the evening and back to her small chamber before she burst into tears. She understood now why Father had always protected her from court life.

She wanted to collect Svetlana and leave here. But where could they go?

CHAPTER 15

*T*he next morning Alyona could not make herself get out of bed. She would make up some excuse about missing breakfast. Lunch, too. After that, she wasn't sure what she would do.

Was she heartbroken? She supposed not, as she had barely known Andrei—Prince Naryshkin. Her father would have called it a silly girl's imaginings, and she supposed that was true. Oh, how she wished for her parents. Her home. She missed it all so much—her mother's boisterous laugh that drew disapproving looks from everyone except her father, her father's adoring gaze when he cast it upon her mother.

Vanya walked into her room without knocking. "I thought I might find you still in bed. You must get up and get dressed for breakfast."

"I do not care for any."

"It doesn't matter. You have to do it. It is imperative. I see that your maid has not yet arrived. I will send mine in to help you."

AS THE TWO WOMEN SAT EATING BREAKFAST A SHORT time later, Alyona said, "How do you live like this? In a place with such scoundrels?"

"Not all men are like that. My fiancé is a good man, and when he returns from Europe, I will introduce you to him and you will understand that I speak the truth. From what you have told me, your father was also proof of that. You just have to be patient until you meet the right sort."

"How am I to know the difference?"

Vanya shrugged. "You must hope for the best, I suppose."

"Somehow that answer is not an encouragement."

Just then, one of the palace maids made her way over to them. "You are Alyona Balashova, yes?"

"I am."

The maid curtsied and handed her a torn piece of paper. There was a hastily inscribed note:

> *Vadim Tchichagov has made arrangements with the empress for*
> *me to return to Kazan with him. I have been notified to pack my*
> *bags and be ready to leave within the hour.*

So that was why Svetlana had not come up to help her get dressed this morning. Alyona looked to the girl who had brought the note. "Where may I find my maid?"

"She is in the servants' hall, packing her things."

"Please tell her that I will come to her as soon as I am able."

The girl curtsied again and hurried off. Alyona looked at Vanya. "The empress has made arrangements with a man so he can take my maid away from here. How is that possible? Svetlana is not a serf. She is not property to be gifted."

"Elizabeth Petrovna is the empress. She can do as she pleases."

"Then I must go to her and change her mind about what it is she pleases."

"The empress spends the first half of her day in her antechambers, where she is not to be disturbed except by invitation. On the day after a ball, she will not emerge until evening."

"I cannot wait until this evening. Svetlana will be gone by then."

Vanya grasped her arm. "The empress fears sleep because she usurped her cousin's throne in the middle of the night. A woman with those kinds of fears will not look with favor or kindness on someone who barges into her chambers when it is expressly forbidden. She will see you as a threat."

"That is a chance I must take."

TWO FINELY DRESSED GUARDS FLANKED THE entrance to the empress's chambers. They each took a step to block the door when Alyona approached. "Her Imperial Majesty is not receiving guests at this hour."

"I am not here on a social call. It is a matter of life and death. I must speak to her. Without delay."

The men glanced at each other. The older one said, "You are General Balashov's daughter, are you not?"

"Yes."

"I fought with your father in the Caucasus. He was a very brave man. I must tell you, though, that even he would not have had the courage to barge into the empress's chambers before she has made ready for guests. Most especially the morning after a ball, when her head throbs from too much drink."

"For the reason I have come, he would. Please, I implore you."

The two guards looked at each other again. The first shrugged. "Your blood be on your own hands." He pulled the door open.

The room inside was mostly dark. The curtains were drawn against the bright sun, although there were a few small candles burning behind amber shades. "Who has entered?"

The voice, while scratchy, could not be mistaken for anyone other than that of the empress. "It is I, Alyona Balashova." The faintest hint of rustling sounded from around the room.

As her eyes adjusted to the dim lighting, Alyona became aware that several people were actually in the chamber. There were servants near the empress, one brushing her hair, one who appeared to be rubbing her feet. Then there was a clump of ladies huddled in the nearest corner. It was obvious from the hints of sparkle that a fair number of jewels adorned them. Thus they would be her closest confidants. They remained perfectly silent, however, without the usual chatter and laughter that would be in this room later in the day. "Come forward, girl."

Her hands shaking, Alyona walked toward the empress. "I am sorry to—"

"Do not speak unless you are spoken to. Do you understand?" The empress's voice had gained volume with her anger.

Alyona dropped her head and nodded meekly. Still, she would not allow herself to be sent from this room without speaking to the empress, whatever it cost her.

"Have the rules of the palace never been explained to you? Apparently, the ladies of the court have failed in their duties." With a wave of her hand, the empress summoned one of the maids of honor forward. "Rectify this oversight immediately."

"The empress is never to be disturbed in her personal

chamber without an express invitation." She paused for a moment. "Never." She gestured toward the door. "Since you are new here, I am certain Her Imperial Majesty understands that this is a mistake of inexperience and lack of training and will not happen again. You may return to her this afternoon when she is in the small salon and beg her forgiveness. For now, you must leave." She extended an arm toward the door.

Alyona fell to her knees. "Please, Your Imperial Majesty. My servant, Svetlana, you have promised her to Vadim Tchichagov, but I beg of you to allow her to stay with me."

An audible gasp burst from the other ladies. The empress shuffled for a moment, then came to her feet. Although it was difficult to see much in the dim lighting, Alyona could see that she had pulled herself to her full height and had her hands clasped in front of her. "You break the rules of your sovereign to ask for the freedom of a mere servant? Is there no limit to your insolence?"

"She is not just a servant; she is my friend. And his intentions are not honorable."

"Bah. Show me a man in all of the Russias whose intentions are honorable when it comes to women."

Alyona leaned forward with her elbows to the floor. "My father's intentions were honorable. Him I would show you if he were still alive." She placed her forehead to the floor and waited for what was to come.

"I will blame your ignorance in approaching me in this manner on your lack of training from your ill-bred mother and your cantankerous father." She stood quietly for a moment, as if considering what next to do, then added, "Although he was a man of honor, this I will concede."

Alyona remained in her prostrate position but did lift her head as the empress sank back into her seat, extended her feet to the servant who had been rubbing them, and gestured toward the woman with the brush to continue. Finally, she said "I think I have a solution that would solve a couple of problems." She gestured to the woman with the brush and said, "Send word that the servant girl is to remain here."

Alyona exhaled the breath she had not realized she was holding. Hope rose from somewhere deep inside her.

Then the empress looked toward her maids of honor. "Send word to Count Vorontsov that I have a solution to his financial problems. And have secured him a bride in the bargain."

*A*lyona and Vanya walked through the garden in silence until they were well past the danger of being overheard. Finally, Alyona said, "What am I to do?"

Vanya shook her head. "I warned you at the ball that you were garnering far too much attention. The empress's jealousy is often swift, but I did not expect action this soon, especially since you were meant for the grand duke's court. I suppose that you forced the decision yourself when you barged into her chambers."

"What else could I do? To wait until later in the day would have meant waiting until it was too late. Had I not acted immediately, Svetlana would already be on her way back to Kazan."

"Yes, that is true. You have saved your maid, but at what cost?"

At what cost indeed? This was the question Alyona had been considering for the past few hours. "How am I to know the cost? I have met Count Vorontsov only briefly. I have no idea what kind of man he is."

"He is a man, almost twenty years your senior, who has

never chosen to marry. Is it worth saving your servant from a lifetime of unhappiness, only to be caught in your own?"

"Who is to say that mine will be a lifetime of unhappiness? My father was twenty-five years older than my mother, and they loved each other dearly. I have seen some young and handsome gentlemen at court who are far less noble than he."

"Then perhaps you have your answer."

WHEN ALYONA RETURNED TO HER ROOM, SHE FOUND Svetlana waiting for her. She fell to the floor and kissed Alyona's feet. "Thank you, mistress, thank you."

Alyona sank to her knees, took Svetlana's face in her hands, and looked her full in the eyes. "This is what friends do. They fight for one another."

Tears streamed down Svetlana's face. "They told me the empress was going to marry you off to some old gaffer. Is it true? Is that what you had to do to save me?"

Alyona pulled her close in an embrace. At this point, it was less about comforting Svetlana and more about disguising her own dismay at the turn of events. "The empress does seek to arrange a marriage between Count Vorontsov and myself."

"Because you went in there this morning to save me? It's all my fault."

Alyona patted the girl on the back. "Who knows what she was planning? My unexpected visit this morning might have sped things up a bit, but Vanya had already told me to be careful and avoid her if possible. The horses were already harnessed to the coach. My visit this morning perhaps provided the crack of a whip, but this runaway carriage was both imminent and inevitable."

Svetlana sniffled and pulled back so she could look at Alyona's face. "What are you going to do?"

"If the empress decides she wants me to wed, then I must wed."

"Surely there must be something."

Alyona clasped her hands. "We can pray."

"Oh, mistress, I shall light every candle in the chapel, then."

Alyona smiled. "I appreciate the thought, although I think one candle and a true outpouring of the heart should be sufficient. Remember what Cook always told us about shipwrecks?"

Svetlana sniffed again and wiped at her nose. "Yes. But that was different."

"How was it different?"

"Well, when she told the story about the apostle Paul's shipwreck on the island that saved all those people and how it was God's plan, our own ships were sailing along just fine. Those stories are better when they are happening to someone else."

Alyona laughed. "In truth, the charm of such stories is quite diminished now that we are the ones on the sinking vessel." She thought about Cook's words, her own mother's similar encouragement during hard times. "The people in those stories weren't happy about their shipwrecks either, but things always worked out for the best. Remember, my own parents' love story began with a troika wreck. Just think what would have happened or, better yet, what wouldn't have happened, if my mother had not crashed that night."

Svetlana nodded and wiped her eyes with the sleeve of her sarafan. "If your mother hadn't come to live in Kazan with your father, Cook would still be a serf and so would all the others, I would likely have starved to death after my parents died, and you would not have been born."

"That is all true. Perhaps this is the man I am supposed to marry. If not, let's pray that God intervenes. Quickly."

"I'm going to light a candle right this instant." Svetlana

hurried out of the room without a backward glance. Alyona did not wait long until she followed. In this case, Svetlana was likely correct. More than one candle might be required.

CHAPTER 17

*T*hat night at dinner, Vanya hurried to Alyona and whispered, "The empress returned to St. Petersburg this morning on some urgent matter. She will be gone for a few weeks, so at least for now, you have a reprieve from whatever is going to happen to you."

A reprieve, yes, but Alyona almost thought the unknown might be worse. Wouldn't it be better to just know what was going to happen and get on with it? "Did you hear, has she been in contact with Count Vorontsov?"

"I am told that she had a missive penned that he was to come to the Winter Palace to speak with her. Whether or not he has received the letter is unknown to me. I believe he travels a great deal."

The next few weeks passed slowly, with Belka and Sabina giggling and whispering every time Alyona was around. She made a point to avoid them and spent long hours walking alone through the breathtaking gardens. One afternoon, a train of magnificent carriages arrived at the palace, followed by wagon after wagon carrying supplies. Alyona sank onto a bench, supposing that the time of her reckoning had come. Only the empress would arrive in a style as opulent as this. Alyona prolonged her walk and went all around the grand pond, stopping to admire the work in progress on the Hermitage Pavilion.

"What do you think of it?" A high-pitched man's voice with a thick German accent came from just behind her.

She whirled around, hand to her throat.

A young man with a badly pockmarked face, wearing full military regalia that dripped with medals and ribbons, laughed at her surprise. A short, heavyset woman held tight to his arm and giggled, as well.

Alyona made a show of fanning her face as she laughed along with them. "Apologies. I did not hear you approach."

"Obviously." He grinned.

Looking at his disfigured face, Alyona could not help but think of her own father. Why had this young man survived smallpox, scarred but still alive, while her father had not? Although her father had been much older, he was a strong man. It was wrong that such a brave man ended that way. Cruel. Unfair.

"Now, back to my question, what do you think of it? Particularly the fake island she had built for the pavilion?" His attire was so fine, he had clearly arrived in the empress's entourage.

Her words needed to be carefully chosen. "I was just pondering the reason for it, sir."

"When the pavilion is complete, she will have a small drawbridge over her own little moat. Thus, she is guaranteed her privacy in her retreat from the main palace."

"She must feel the need for privacy very keenly if she goes to such lengths to obtain it."

"Yes, she does. There will be mechanical tables installed, so the waiters will not need to be in the room. The plates will simply disappear down a tube and arrive back up with the appropriate food already on them."

"You are teasing me."

He put his hand on his heart. "On my honor, it is all true. My aunt likes to be in control of who is, and who is not, around her."

His aunt? She curtsied low. "Forgive me for my ignorance, Your Imperial Highness. I did not realize to whom I was speaking." Her heart fluttered inside her chest. Once again, she was certain she was not handling this according to royal propriety, but once again, she had no idea what that propriety involved.

"Yes, yes." He waved his hand dismissively. "And may I present Elizaveta Vorontsova."

Alyona curtsied toward the woman. Why was she walking with the grand duke? Where was Grand Duchess Catherine? Then she remembered the rumors of his affair.

The grand duke said, "Tell us, what is your name?"

"Alyona Arkadyevna Balashova, Your Imperial Highness."

"Ah, the general's daughter." The grand duke nodded with approval. "He was a great military tactician. Not as great as Frederick of Prussia, but still, a wise military leader. Russia needs more of his kind."

"I seem to recall that I was told that you would be joining our number at Oranienbaum. Is this not true?" Elizaveta cocked her head to the side and studied her.

"That was to be the plan. However, the empress has recently expressed the desire that I marry instead, so I am uncertain of my future path." Only then did it occur to her this woman's last name. "His name is Count Vorontsov. Are you related?"

"Lev Vorontsov?"

"Yes."

Elizaveta sighed deeply. "He is my cousin." She rolled her eyes up at the grand duke and shook her head. "I wonder what she is thinking in arranging such a match?"

"She is thinking there will be a wedding and she will dance and dance and dance." Peter pranced around in a circle, kicking his feet from side to side. They both laughed, but Alyona could not bring herself to join in.

Elizaveta beckoned her forward. "Come, walk with us back to the palace. We brought entertainment in our entourage, and they should almost be done setting up by now. You'll not want to miss the dancing monkeys. They are quite hysterical."

The three of them walked back together, with Elizaveta speaking in such a boisterous voice that spittle often flew from her mouth, seeming to punctuate the curses and vulgarities that flowed with regularity.

These coarse manners reminded Alyona of the stories of her own mother, but her mother had been a shopkeeper's daughter who had educated herself and would never have spoken with such foulness. This woman, born into a noble family and apparently held in high regard by the grand duke of Russia, seemed to delight in her flagrant disregard of proper behaviors. Still, it was nice to be around someone who wasn't false and backbiting, like Belka and Sabina.

Outside the palace, a makeshift stage had been assembled and servants were bringing out chairs and tables, along with platters of fruits and cheese. "Please, Alyona, come sit with me."

"Of course." Alyona followed Elizaveta, expecting her to release the arm of the grand duke and go sit with other members of the court. This did not happen, however, and she walked up to the table of honor and waited for a servant to pull back her chair, directly beside the grand duke's. Alyona backed up a step. "I... surely it would not be appropriate for me to sit here?"

"Appropriate? We care little for such things. Life is about enjoying it, and that is what is appropriate." Elizaveta looked at the grand duke. "Is that not right, darling?"

Darling? This woman was openly referring to the grand duke as darling? Alyona glanced nervously over her shoulder. When might the grand duchess appear, and what would she have to say about all this?

"Yes. Sit. I want to hear all about your father. What was he like off the battlefield? Did he enjoy practicing military drills as much as I do?"

"Honestly, it was like speaking to the young boys in Kazan who used to follow my father around. Lots of talk of battlefields and bravery but not much common sense to accompany it." Alyona was thankful for Svetlana's presence as she dressed for dinner. She could speak freely without worrying about repercussions. "And since the empress slighted my father and mother because of his outspoken behavior and my mother's lack of breeding, I find it hard to believe that she approves of the grand duke's...friend, in spite of the fact she is from a noble family."

"The maids say she can curse better than the soldiers."

"As if cursing 'better' is a goal one would wish to attain." Alyona shook her head. "Court is nothing at all like I dreamed it would be. I see now why my father avoided it."

"It makes me wonder what it would have been like if he were here now. Would you see things differently?" Svetlana held one section of braid under her chin as she twirled together another piece.

"Perhaps. And perhaps I would be meeting a different element of the court because I would have Father here to protect me. Still..." Alyona sighed and thought her heart might break. "Remember how mother used to take food to the prisoners? It always embarrassed me. As I look back on my attitude toward her charity, I am ashamed of myself. So very ashamed. I did not want the fancy people to scoff at me for doing something so lowly. I see it so clearly now. I was seeking the approval of the wrong people."

Svetlana tucked the two braids together, then reached for a length of ribbon. "They're not all bad. These fancy people."

"True. Vanya is quite kind. I believe it is because she comes from a good family and is already betrothed. Since it is a love match, but also with good connections, she doesn't feel the need to compete with anyone else."

"Compete. Yes. That's what these women do. It is sad, really." Svetlana wrapped the blue ribbon around the knot of braids. "Mightn't the grand duke and his friend take you back with them? To Oranienbaum? That would be one way to escape an arranged marriage."

Alyona toyed with the ivory-handled hairbrush on the table before her, turning it over and over in her hands. "I had hoped for this, as well. Unfortunately, they are leaving here for Moscow. By the time they return, it will be too late, I fear." She set the brush back on the bureau. "I wonder what kind of people associate with Count Vorontsov? Hopefully some of the nicer ones."

"You will still have me, yes, and I am nice."

Alyona reached up and squeezed her hands. "And I am grateful for that." And she was grateful, but oh how she hoped for more.

CHAPTER 18

November 1752
Tsarskoe Selo, Russia

The empress did not return for the remainder of the summer, leaving Alyona to wonder at her fate. As each week and then month passed, her hopes grew that this arranged marriage might not occur. When word came that only the closest members of court were to return to the Winter Palace and the rest were to remain at Catherine Palace through Christmas, her hope truly surged. Might she yet be attached to the court of the grand duke and duchess and be allowed to stay with them?

One day while Svetlana was doing a fitting for Alyona's newest gown, she was chatting away as usual. "There must be an extra-special guest coming to dinner tonight. The maids and kitchen staff were all in an uproar."

"I can't imagine who it will be. It seems that most people of any importance are in the city now. It's only the lesser courtiers still in Tsarskoe Selo, and no one would visit this close to the Nativity Fast."

A knock came at the door. "Come in." Alyona turned and saw a maid she did not recognize.

"Her Imperial Majesty requests your presence in her chambers immediately after tea tomorrow afternoon."

Alyona looked at Svetlana. She knew now what all the scurry had been about. "Thank you. I shall be there." Alyona watched the girl leave, her stomach tightening. "I suppose my future is about to be set before me."

Svetlana nodded and stuck in the final pin. "I pray that it's a good one."

Alyona reached up and took her hand. "For both of us."

When Alyona entered the room, the empress looked up and smiled, her expression as delighted as if she were seeing an old friend. "Come, Alyona Arkadyevna, please, take a seat here beside me."

Empress Elizabeth was clad in a pale-green silk gown with red birds embroidered all around the skirt, each with a startling blue eye of lapis lazuli. Her countenance seemed more relaxed than Alyona could ever remember seeing it. It reminded Alyona of her father after the Christmas feast, when he would recline, hand on his stomach, declaring he could not possibly want for one more thing in his entire life. When he wore this expression, everyone understood it was the time to ask him for favors.

"I have spoken the wish to have you wed to Count Vorontsov. He has always been a favorite of mine, and I have long wished for him to settle down and produce legitimate heirs."

The word *legitimate* was not lost on Alyona. She could only assume this meant that there were children of the other variety. This thought had never crossed her mind before, and it caused her to recoil.

"Count Vorontsov, it turns out, wishes to speak with you before agreeing to this marriage." The fact that he could make that choice, told Alyona just how much of a favorite he truly was. "He should arrive at any moment now."

Alyona remained silent, except her heart that was about to pound out of her chest. Her entire life would be decided in the next few hours.

The empress watched her evenly and then nodded, as if pleased by the fact that Alyona had the sense not to say anything. "I will tell you the bargain I have struck."

"I would appreciate that, Your Imperial Majesty."

"I own an estate a few hours west of here. I gifted it to a nobleman I held in high regard who has since moved to Moscow and passed away. He had no heirs, so the estate is once again back in my hands. There is precious little land attached to the manor house, and therefore it has always been expensive and difficult to maintain.

"The home alone is worth twice the value of your father's in Kazan. As a show of my appreciation for his service, I am prepared to transfer ownership of this home to you as a wedding gift. As for the money from the sale of your home in Kazan, I shall gift it to Count Vorontsov as your dowry, and with that, he may purchase one thousand desyatina in the surrounding area, which I will sell to him at a bargain price. It would make the estate self-supporting, you would be the undisputed owner of the house, therefore you would be able to keep your maid as you see fit. I believe you place great value on the creature."

Just then, Count Vorontsov was led into the room. He bowed low. "Good afternoon, Your Imperial Majesty." He was richly dressed, with gold braiding on his epaulets, and wearing a fine shirt.

"Now, dear Count Vorontsov, please look at this beautiful girl who is seated beside me and tell me you do not believe she would make an excellent wife."

He looked at Alyona and nodded. "Any man would be lucky to claim her, Your Imperial Majesty."

"Exactly. So, let us begin wedding preparations, shall we? Since I owe both you and Alyona's father a great debt, I have chosen your wedding celebration to be the very first in the new Smolny Cathedral. Monsieur Rastrelli assures me it will be ready to host ceremonies the day before the fast begins, exactly as I had hoped."

"I would like to speak to the young lady privately for a few moments."

"There will be plenty of time for talk after the wedding."

"Your Majesty, I have many vices, as you and I are both well aware. One of those vices, however, has never been to take a woman against her will. I would like to think I can leave this earth with one piece of my honor still intact."

Elizabeth made a dismissive gesture. "She is young. You will teach her what her will is."

Again, he said, "I need to speak with her in private."

"Very well. But be quick about it."

Alyona followed him from the room, her knees trembling. To her surprise, he did not stop in the hallway to speak but instead led her outside, in spite of the freezing temperature. She crossed her arms in front of herself, shivering from...cold? Or fear?

He gestured toward the building. "There are fewer ears out here."

"I understand."

"Alyona Arkadyevna, I will admit that I depend upon the empress's good humor for my livelihood, and her good humor has been intent upon getting me married and producing heirs.

For myself, I have never sought marriage nor desired it, but I will admit that as I have grown older, I have begun to long for an heir and a namesake. However, other than the empress demanding it be so, I can see no reason why you would desire this marriage. Yes, I am of the nobility and carry a title, but most of my money has long since gone. There can be little benefit to you in a title alone, and a young woman of your beauty could definitely find other more desirable suitors. As I said to the empress, I do not want a woman by force, be it my own or the empress's."

He stopped speaking and waited for her response. He must have seen that she was shivering but made no offer of his coat— a failure that her father would have viewed in a negative light. "Well, sir, in complete truth this was not a union I sought, nor had I sought for any to be so soon." She paused and thought about what was at stake. "I came to the court with many dreams, but none of it has been as I expected."

He stroked his beard. "Why she chose this particular union at this particular time I confess myself perplexed."

"I believe I can enlighten you. The fault lies with me. During the summer, I barged into her antechambers after a ball and begged her to save my maid. Her decision to see me married happened at that moment."

"Save your maid?"

Alyona told him the story, he nodded and looked at her with renewed interest. "I know that the empress has offered to sell you land for much less money than it is worth, but I do believe that it would destroy my very soul if I were to live in a place where serfs worked the land."

He nodded, still pulling at his beard. "I remember now. Your parents freed all their serfs, did they not?"

"Yes, it was my mother's requirement of my father before she would agree to marry him."

He stared off into the bleakness of an early winter day, with no snow as yet to cover up the withered plants left behind after their glorious summer. "Angering the empress is in neither of our best interests. However, I have a plan that should give us more time. She is looking for a wedding before the Nativity Fast because it gives an excuse for a lavish party. She also wants to show off Monsieur Rastrelli's design on the new cathedral. If we can concoct a reason to postpone, it will defeat her purpose on both counts." He tapped the fingers of his hands together as he thought. "I have an upcoming trip and will suggest that we arrange our nuptials for perhaps the spring. She will find another wedding to fit her plans, and by the time spring is here, our arrangement will long be forgotten."

Alyona almost fainted with relief. "Will she forget?"

He brushed at something on his jacket. "She has a short memory, unless her anger or jealousy has been aroused. You need to avoid notice whenever possible."

"I will do so."

He lifted her chin so she could look him in the eyes. "You are too innocent to survive long at court. I hope that you find a way out, somewhere you can remain true to who you are." He turned then and led her back inside.

When they reentered the antechamber, it was obvious the empress was engaged in a heated conversation in spite of the fact that her voice was too low to hear. A short, fat man stood nodding, and listening, and trying to interject, although she cut him off at every attempt. Finally, she stood and pointed her finger directly into the man's face. "If I ever—" before specifying the exact nature of the threat, she noticed Alyona and the count standing in the doorway and motioned toward one of her servants. "Get him out of my sight." The man was escorted from the room, and she gestured them forward.

"Your Imperial Majesty, I speak for both of us when I say what an incredible honor it is that you have chosen such a wonderful match for each of us. We can think of nothing that would delight us more than to claim the first wedding celebration in the new Smolny Cathedral.

"However, I have already made arrangements for my annual trip to the Urals during the fast. As the priests will not marry anyone from the fast through Christmas and then on through the weeks of Theophany, we would like to wait to pursue our nuptials in the spring."

"You have planned travel during the Nativity Fast? This is unheard of."

He stroked his beard and shrugged roguishly. "As you know, Your Majesty, I have never been a pious person, and forty days of no meat or strong drink is a tradition I prefer to avoid. I have found this a most beneficial time to undertake business travels in the mining area."

She laughed outright at this. "Yes, I suppose that you would." She thought for a moment. "We shall plan the wedding for the day before the fast."

"Your Imperial Majesty, I appreciate your haste, however, Alyona Arkadyevna is young and innocent. The Ural Mountains in winter is not a fit place for any woman, so I could not possibly take her with me."

A palace cat jumped up in her lap, and the empress stroked it, her eyes narrowed in concentration. "Yes, I see that there is truth in that. An innocent young bride requires lots of undivided attention." She studied Alyona for a moment and nodded. "Yes, that is how it must be."

Count Vorontsov bowed. "I thank you, Majesty, for your understanding in this matter."

"Yes, I do understand." She set the cat aside, stood, and walked over to Alyona, the silk of her skirt rustling as she walked. She rubbed Alyona's cheek with the back of her hand. After her last finger had trailed off, she said, "We shall plan the wedding for the day before the fast."

"But Majesty—"

The empress cut him off with an upraised hand. "After the celebration, she shall return to her chambers here and you shall depart on your trip. Not until you return from your travels will the marriage be consummated, but the ceremony will happen the night before the fast begins—the first in the new Smolny Cathedral, just as I have willed it. I will personally see to preparations for the wedding."

Alyona could not breathe. There was nothing she could do but wait for Count Vorontsov to devise another argument. He bowed again. "I thank you for the honor, Majesty."

With that, he led Alyona from the room. After the door closed behind them, he reached for her hand and kissed it. "Until I see you again."

And just like that, Alyona's life had been decided.

CHAPTER 19

"The day of your wedding. I would have thought we would have been running around crazy, but since Her Imperial Majesty made all the plans, I've barely had a thing to do except fix this up for you." Svetlana fluffed up a white velvet sleeve, then fluffed it some more. "And she gave you one of her own dresses."

"One of her own dresses that she has worn previously," Alyona looked down at the embroidery on her neckline, "and then proceeded to cut out the jewels that had been sewn in."

"It's strange that she insisted on you wearing one of her old dresses instead of allowing you to make your own. And stranger still that she, who demands no one wear the same ball gown twice, gives away her used dresses and insists that you wear it—to your wedding, no less. They say she often does it to her favorite servants, but you're not a servant. It's odd."

"Perhaps not quite so odd." Alyona knew the empress had never favored her. "It's a good thing you are so skilled at embroidery so you can cover up all the holes the jewels left behind. No one will be any the wiser."

Svetlana stood back and appraised the gown, then nodded with satisfaction. "I wonder what they'll serve at the wedding feast."

A knock sounded at the door, and Vanya opened it. "May I come in?"

"Of course. I'm delighted to see you, dear friend." It was the first time the two women had seen each other since Vanya's own wedding several months ago.

"And I, you." She proceeded to walk a full circle around Alyona. "You look beautiful."

"Thank you. It's all Svetlana's doing."

Vanya smiled. "She definitely has a good eye for needlework."

Svetlana's cheeks turned red at the compliment. "I wish I could have made a proper dress. A new one, not a hand-me-down."

"The gift of Empress Elizabeth's dresses is considered an honor."

"By her, maybe," Svetlana whispered under her breath.

Vanya's eyes widened in silent acknowledgment. "Just be grateful that there were only some holes to be mended. In the heat of the summer, these dresses are often sweat stained from a summer night's dancing. It is almost impossible to remove the stains, or the smell, from a gown like this."

Svetlana wrinkled up her nose. "I suppose I am thankful for that then."

Vanya turned to Alyona. "How are you feeling about today? The wedding?"

Alyona shrugged. "I admit to being nervous about how it will all work out, but I am determined to make the best of this situation. There must be some reason that God has brought us all together. I will trust Him, as my mother and Cook always taught me."

"There are few I know who would speak of wisdom gained from their cook."

"That is because they have not had the privilege of knowing my cook."

"Exactly." Again, Svetlana puffed the words under her breath so they were almost impossible to hear.

Vanya cocked her head to the side. "What of your groom? How is he feeling about everything?"

This question touched on Alyona's greatest fear. "I do not know."

"What do you mean you do not know? You spoke to him yesterday, upon your arrival in St. Petersburg, surely?"

Alyona shook her head. "No."

"He has written you perhaps?"

Again she shook her head. "I have not heard from him since our meeting with the empress, almost a fortnight ago." She did not tell Vanya that he, too, had been hoping to get out of this wedding. Since it was common knowledge that all letters from or to the court were seen by many eyes, no good could come out of plotting their deliverance via means the empress would certainly know about. "I am certain he has been busy preparing for his journey to the Ural Mountains. He is to leave St. Petersburg this very evening."

"Truly? I assumed that to be a rumor."

"No. I am to return here and live in this room until such a time as he returns to St. Petersburg. I do not know when that will be, exactly, but sometime after Theophany."

"But that is almost two months hence."

"Yes."

"In that case then, I particularly hope that your mother and cook were correct in their teaching. Otherwise, I am frightened for your future."

Alyona did not speak for fear of voicing the truth and making it more real. She, too, was frightened. So much so that she was not certain how she would make it through this day.

THE EMPRESS RODE IN THE SLEIGH BESIDE ALYONA, adorned in a gown of sapphire blue with white fur trimming the arms and neckline. The fact that she wore European attire, and not a sarafan, proclaimed a level of respect Alyona had not expected. "I have long been in Count Vorontsov's debt. I am thankful that today, I may discharge that burden."

Alyona wondered at the appropriate reply to being told that she was being bartered away to ease the empress's sense of owing—to someone who did not want the gift being offered. She knew that nothing would be acceptable except humility. "I am honored that you have chosen me."

The empress clasped her gloved hand. "Your father would be proud. His daughter wed to a nobleman of such high esteem in the court."

"Yes, Your Imperial Majesty."

The sleigh arrived at the cathedral, which sat in the midst of a convent, all of which were still under some level of construction. The structure was beautiful, in the Baroque style so favored by the empress. The exterior was the palest of blues, and the trim white—very similar to the Catherine Palace, without all the ostentatious gold trim, this being reserved for the crosses that rose atop the onion spires.

Alyona made her way inside, her whole body trembling. Still, she moved forward, shoulders back, head held high, just as her father had taught her.

Count Vorontsov was there waiting for her. He smiled, his

eyes kind, and the ceremony proceeded. The crowns were held over their heads, chants made, and prayers given. Several hours later, they emerged from the chapel as man and wife.

The two of them rode back to the Winter Palace in the wedding sleigh, pulled by a team of white horses, bells jingling on their harnesses. Count Vorontsov reached over and took her hand, but he said nothing. When they arrived at the palace, a footman helped them alight from the sleigh, and they were led to the great hall.

As the evening progressed, the empress did indeed change into a peasant's sarafan before she led out the opening dance, just as Alyona had been told she liked to do at her arranged weddings. The count took Alyona's hand and led her to the dance floor. "I make no pretensions of being anything close to an honorable man. However, as we have been joined in matrimony, I shall do my best to behave in a manner more worthy. More than that, I cannot promise."

Certainly not the words a girl dreamed of hearing on her wedding day. Still, given the circumstances, Alyona took the declaration for the gift it was. "I thank you. I, too, shall do my best to be a worthy companion, Count Vorontsov."

"Countess Vorontsova, you are my wife now, and therefore must call me Lev. As for your response to my statement, it is in no way fair." He twirled her around.

"Not fair?"

"All you will need to do is continue to be the woman you are. I, however, will need to change almost everything about the man I am."

"I am certain you exaggerate your weaknesses, sir."

"I wish that were the case, but in all honesty, I must state most emphatically that it is not."

They danced without words for a while, but the silence felt companionable, as if they were each trying to learn to navigate this new story they had been written into. When the music ended for the last song, he cupped her cheek. "You are so beautiful. I look forward to my return and the start of our true life together." He leaned forward and kissed her gently on the lips, then turned and walked out the door.

CHAPTER 20

The palace celebrated the Nativity in perfect Orthodox manner, which included forty days of fasting and prayer on the weeks leading up to Christmas. While Elizabeth by no means lived a pure life, she feared the fires of hell and did everything possible to curry God's good favor.

"Remember how your father used to get so angry about the Nativity Fast?" Svetlana said as she braided Alyona's hair for the Christmas Eve dinner.

"How could anyone not remember that?" This memory of her father was bittersweet, as were so many things these days. "I can still hear him saying it was an affront to the Christ child to fast before His arrival. The fast during Lent, of course, was quite a different matter since it ended with the crucifixion and should be mourned."

"I think he might be right." Svetlana inserted a hairpin, "but do not tell the priests I said so."

For Christmas Eve, the entire court had attended the Royal Hours and Vespers at the Smolny Cathedral. Walking back into that place brought so many emotions. Alyona had been married in this very room some forty days ago. Her husband had gone on a journey and she had yet to hear from him, and had no idea when he might return. She found that each new day brought a greater fear than the day before of what her life might be. Count Vorontsov had always been kind to her, but that was before he had been forced into a marriage he did not desire.

Once the services were over, the court returned to the Winter Palace. In the traditional way, they found hay scattered on the floor and tables to symbolize Christ's manger, a white tablecloth to symbolize His swaddling clothes, and a tall white candle in the middle of the table to remind all present that Christ is the light of the world.

As waiters brought out the twelve dishes, made to symbolize the twelve apostles, Alyona found herself fighting back tears. Christmas had always been such a rich and meaningful time with her family. She could remember well how much care her mother had always taken with these preparations. Now, her parents were gone, and Alyona was married to a stranger.

At the stroke of midnight, the priests walked around the church to celebrate the arrival of the Savior. Afterwards, the court returned to their rooms to rest up for the large Christmas feast the next day. Alyona buried her head in her pillow and cried.

At some point in the middle of the night, she rose and went to the icon corner in her room. She lit a candle and prayed. "Forgive me for being ungrateful for the many blessings that are mine. Please help all the servants from my home in Kazan to stay safe and warm and well fed. And would You please send me a sign—anything—just some sort of token to show me that You hear me?" This was likely and impudent prayer, but Cook had always said there's no reason to pretend anything with God, as He knows the truth about everything anyway.

After a long time of pouring out her heart, she blew out the candle and returned to her bed. "Thank You, Father, for the gift of Christmas."

Then she rolled over and fell asleep.

"MISTRESS, WAKE UP. MISTRESS, WAKE UP."

Alyona opened her eyes to find her maid's face barely an inch from her own. "Svetlana? What's happened?"

"Word has come, mistress. We must go. Yes, yes. Go now."

"What word?"

"The master. He arrived at the estate yesterday and wants us there immediately."

"Immediately? Surely we will wait until after we have celebrated the Christmas feast." She looked toward the window. "It is still dark outside."

"His servant is downstairs in the great hall and has everyone in an uproar." Svetlana grasped her hand and pulled, trying to force Alyona to get up.

"All right, all right." She sat up and rubbed her eyes, still heavy with fatigue. "Let's take extra care with preparations. If it is to be my first day with my husband, I do not want to look a mess."

"Yes, yes, I've already got your outfit sorted out. Two of the palace maids will be here at any moment to help us pack."

Alyona moved as quickly as possible, and Svetlana was moving even faster. Within half an hour, they were climbing into the vozok, which had already been warmed by the furnace. It was the finest winter carriage Alyona had ever seen, with seats lined in dark burgundy velvet, and the windows covered by a heavy satin drape in the same color.

"Isn't this fancy?" Svetlana said as she climbed up beside her.

"The most amazing vozok I have ever seen, for sure."

"His Excellency requires nothing but the best." The male servant, who had not spoken to them thus far but instead had barked orders at everyone nearby when Alyona and Svetlana arrived downstairs, squinted, then lifted little round spectacles to his eyes. He bowed his head toward Alyona. "My name is Pavel, and I am His Excellency's valet. The ride to Taitsy will take two to three hours, depending on the road conditions. Try to get some rest." After that, Pavel looked at his fingernails, scowled at Svetlana, then leaned his head against the cushions. Within minutes he was snoring.

Svetlana stared at him and rolled her eyes. "He sure makes a lot of noise for such a fancy man."

Alyona stifled the nervous giggle that rose to her throat. And she was nervous. Terrified.

She pulled the curtain back. Although the sun had not risen, the snow still reflected the dim light of the retreating moon and stars. They crossed over the frozen Neva River and were soon on their way to the unknown.

Alyona looked across the vast blanket of white and tried to think about Cook and her shipwreck analogy. And her mother and her troika wreck. Surely all of this was part of God's plan. But if that were the case, why was it so terrifying?

CHAPTER 21

"We will be arriving in a few minutes. Perhaps you will want to gather yourself." Pavel's voice jerked Alyona awake. She opened her eyes to find him staring out the small window near him.

Svetlana was still asleep, curled up in a ball on the padded seat, her face a picture of serenity. How Alyona envied that.

She pulled back the heavy drapes beside her to get her bearings, although in doing so, a draft of cold emanated from the windows. The light caused Svetlana to stir. She sat up straight and stretched her arms above her head and yawned. She then turned toward Alyona. "Where are we?"

"We just entered Taitsy. The gated entrance to the estate is just a versta ahead now," Pavel replied.

"Well then, let me see what we need to adjust." Svetlana stood. "This is one of those times it is nice to be so short, yes, yes. Most people would have to double over in here." She examined Alyona's hair, tucking in a few strays. "You look beautiful. Yes. Beautiful."

Alyona most certainly did not feel beautiful. She felt rumpled and disheveled after the journey. Still, she pinched her cheeks a few times to bring up some color.

The iron gates that opened to the estate were imposing but not pretentious. An orchard lined the sides of the driveway leading up to the house. Although the trees were barren now, Alyona could imagine how beautiful this looked in the spring and summer.

Her heart began to pound. The rectangular two-story house was pale yellow trimmed in white, with a small balcony above the front door. A perfect blend of lovely and understated. She knew immediately it would feel like home.

As they made their way up the circular drive, a clump of people emerged from the side of the house. They were dressed in festive colors, clearly prepared for the celebration of Christmas. The front door opened, and Lev walked out and stood there in a fine suit, his hands clasped behind his back, flanked by servants on each side.

"It can't be." Svetlana pressed her face against the window on Pavel's side of the carriage, much to his obvious displeasure. "But it is. That is Cook. And Tikhon. And Betsy."

"What?" Alyona could not believe it. All the servants from their home in Kazan lined the driveway to greet them. The sight of them all safe—and here—filled her with equal measures of joy and relief. What a blessing!

The vozok came to a stop, and Lev himself opened the door and extended a hand for Alyona to climb down. "Welcome to your new home, Countess Vorontsova."

Her gloved hand held tight to his as she made her way down the steps. Otherwise, she didn't think her knees would support her. "I thank you." She gestured toward the assembled servants. "Am I to believe what I am seeing?"

He smiled and nodded. "You told me of your disdain for the practice of serfdom. I made some inquiries and learned of the plight of your former servants. I thought perhaps it would help ease you into this new life if you could be surrounded by people with whom you were already familiar."

She shook her head back and forth, still not believing what she was seeing. "You could not have given me a better gift."

He squeezed her hand and, with a twinkle in his eye, said, "Perhaps then I should return my other wedding gifts. And the Christmas gifts as well."

"You could do so, and I promise you my heart would still burst with joy. That said, there is no reason to be hasty." They both laughed, and it reminded her of his sense of humor and how she had enjoyed his company.

Meanwhile, Svetlana had climbed down from the carriage. She looked toward the familiar crowd in the driveway and snorted. "Aren't we living large now?"

Cook scowled. "Some of us more than others apparently. Here you come, riding in the vozok with the mistress like you are someone important."

Svetlana threw her shoulders back and raised herself to her full height, which was still shoulder high to anyone else in the crowd. "Yes, I am someone important. I am. I spent the last months in Her Imperial Majesty's palace, I did. Let's see any of *you* top that." She crossed her arms and made a triumphant *hmph*.

"This one believes that she is sitting well now." Cook shook her head, then gestured toward the side of the house. "Get yourself to the kitchen. We are in the midst of preparing the Christmas feast and need every set of useful hands."

Svetlana nodded sharply, smiled, and made her way around the house, followed by the rest of the servants. Lev led Alyona inside. "Merry Christmas."

A staircase stood just past the foyer. It was festooned with evergreen boughs, and a candlelit tree glowed in the drawing room just to the right. Everything about it felt so warm, so welcoming.

Lev took her hand and showed her around the house, which was lovely. They went upstairs and he showed her their room, which was also decorated with evergreens and candles. "It's beautiful."

"I am glad you think so." As if sensing her nervousness, he squeezed her hand and quickly moved on.

Next to their bedchamber, a nursery was already established and furnished with every thoughtful detail. "I thought it would give you comfort to have our baby nearby, but if you prefer, we can move it to the end of the hall."

"Oh no, you were exactly correct. I will want my children near to me."

He nodded and smiled with satisfaction. "I thought as much." He led her out onto the balcony, walked over to the railing, and gestured to the land around them. "I plan to make something of this place. We have plenty of grazing and farm land to the back and west of the house. I am going to endeavor to be a better man than I have ever been." He put his hands on her shoulders and gazed deep into her eyes. "Do you think you can be happy here? With me? Can you try?"

Alyona looked back at the man who had just found a safe home for every one of her father's former servants. She knew then that this shipwreck had indeed been the work of God all along.

She put her hand on his arm. "Indeed, I do not believe there is another place or person in all of the Russias that could make me as happy as I am now."

He pulled her into his arms and kissed her, very gently, then he leaned back to smile into her eyes. "Welcome to your new home, Countess."

And at that moment, she knew it. She was home.

Svetlana came barreling up the stairs. "Cook says the Christmas feast is ready to begin." She bounced up and down a few times, hands clasped before her. "It looks divine."

Lev nodded in a very dignified manner. "Please tell Cook that we are on our way to the table."

"Yes, I will." Svetlana bounded down the stairs, waiting until she reached near the bottom before shouting, "The master and mistress are on their way."

Lev extended his arm for Alyona to take. He leaned closer and whispered, "If your maid is any indication, I believe that we are about to partake in the happiest Christmas in all of the Russias."

"I believe you might be correct."

"Perhaps when the feast is done, I shall take you on a troika ride to survey the property."

"I would love that."

"Did you not tell me your parents met on a troika ride?"

Such a small detail. The fact that he remembered it sent a flood of warmth through her. "A troika crash, but yes."

"A crash, hm?" He pulled at his beard and smiled at her. "I will try my best not to reenact that particular part of the event."

"Do not be so hasty. It seems that sometimes a wreck is required to get us where we need to go."

"If that is how you feel, then I shall see to it that our troika crashes in a most spectacular fashion."

"I can hardly wait."

The End

QUESTIONS FOR CONVERSATION

1) Were you surprised to find a woman ruling as empress /tsarina in 18th century Russia? Did anything about the 18th century Russian court surprise you?

2) Were you expecting this to be more of a light-hearted romance? How did you feel about this different kind of Christmas novella?

3) Svetlana had no choice when she was to be sent to work for the colonel's son. Alyona realized that she was also powerless to save her maid "without a strong champion like her father." Do you see yourself, or other people/people groups as being as helpless as Svetlana, even in today's world? What is required to be a strong champion—money, fame, the loudest voice? Can you identify a strong champion in your own life? Have you ever been someone else's strong champion?

4) When Alyona first met Grand Duke Peter she noticed his pock-marked face and knew that he had survived smallpox—the disease that killed her father. She was struck by the unfairness of it all. Do you struggle with the unfair things that have happened to you? Are there good things that have happened that are also unfair?

5) Alyona reflects back on being ashamed of her mother taking food to the prisons. She says, "I see it so clearly now, I was seeking the approval of the wrong people." Are there things you should be doing that you don't, because you would feel embarrassed? Do you do things you should not, to gain others' approval? Is it possible to be doing "good" things and it still be wrong because it is done for the wrong reason or outside of your own true calling?

6) Empress Elizabeth was known for her fasting, praying and religious pilgrimages, yet she was also known for a life of excess, promiscuity, and narcissism. How do you think these things can co-exist in one person? Do you think there is a modern version of this in our society today?

7) The "storms and shipwrecks" motto is based on the apostle Paul's shipwreck onto Malta recounted in Acts 27 and 28. Paul's presence there resulted in the gospel being spread and many sick people being healed. Can you think of a time in your life that seemed like a shipwreck, but you look back on it now and see that it truly worked for good?

8) How did you feel about the arranged wedding? Do you believe that Alyona and Count Vorontsov will have a happy marriage? What leads you to such a conclusion?

ACKNOWLEDGMENTS

Lee, Melanie, and Caroline Cushman- Every single day I am grateful that I get to be part of such an amazing family. Also, thanks for accompanying me on my dream trip around the Baltic Sea, which spawned the desire to write historical fiction in Imperial Russia. Thanks for humoring me in my dinner dissertations about Russian history, my online Russian language classes, and the Russian folk music blasting through the house while I'm writing.

SAFS book club- Stacey, Rachel, Jamie, Kat, and Emily—What a privilege to speak monthly with friends from multiple countries who share a love of reading and Russian history. You are an amazing group of women. I hope we all meet in person someday.

Kathleen—For being a true friend, wise advisor, and fun travel buddy.

Alisa Parrish- Your strength and courage have always inspired me, never more than this year. You are a true hero in every sense of the word.

Carl Parrish- for being an encourager, friend, helper, and very close approximation of Pops (the praise could not get any higher than this).

Judy and Denice- our little zoom Bible study has been such a blessing over the past couple of years. Thank you for keeping me grounded.

Brenna, Lisa, and Susie- A bedrock of friendship, and great pickleball partners too.

Mike and Lisa Champion- stalwart friends through life's hard times.

The Goodland Book Club- Genessa, Shannon, Christy, Nikki, Christine, Leora, Cindy, Keely, Amy, Nancy, and Robyn. Thank you for loving the written word as much as I do, and reminding me why I do this. What an amazing group of women you are.

Julee Schwarzburg- Thank you making the big picture so much clearer in these stories.

Carrie Padgett- For cleaning up the final product, offering encouragement, and generally being a lifelong friend.

Stacey Watson- Thank you for reading through the manuscript and helping make it more authentically Russian.

Torrey Lind- For designing the little vozok and troika to separate the scenes. Thanks for taking my random ideas and turning them into exactly what I need.

Most of all- thank You Heavenly Father for carrying me through those times when it has seemed impossible to take one more step forward on my own.

THE CHRISTMAS GIFT

To Stacey, Rachel, and Jamie—your lives were upended through no fault of your own. Yet you all keep smiling, keep loving those around you, and keep moving forward, even though the next step must be so incredibly difficult sometimes. You will never know how much you inspire me

CHAPTER 1

May 1753
Taitsy, Russia

"*H*ave you made certain all the count's medals and badges are packed precisely as specified? Have you checked everything a second time?" Countess Alyona Vorontsova looked toward her young maid, Svetlana, who nodded vigorously.

"Oh yes, yes. A second and a third time and even a fourth. His Excellency has been in such a good mood about the trip to Peterhof Palace, I didn't want anything to spoil it. No, I did not."

Lev was indeed delighted about the journey ahead. Although he had not said so, Alyona knew he had grown restless here. Thirty-eight years of living as a carefree bachelor in the middle of St. Petersburg provided a stark contrast to life on a country estate with a new wife he had not chosen.

Now, his valet had fallen ill, so the duty of packing his trunks had landed on Svetlana. She had taken to the task with characteristic good humor. Alyona attempted to assist, even if neither of them knew exactly how to prepare his things. The invitation lay open on Lev's bedside table:

Empress Elizabeth Petrovna
requests the honor
of the Count and Countess Vorontsov
Peterhof Palace
May 7–May 28

"I cannot believe we are going to Peterhof. I can hardly wait to see all the gorgeous ball gowns and hear all the enchanting music." Svetlana twirled around and pretended to bow to a dance partner. "It seems forever since we were at court. This will be thrilling, yes?"

Alyona sighed. "I am most looking forward to meeting Grand Duchess Catherine. I have always believed we will be friends. It is silly, I suppose, as I have never met her."

"It is because the grand duke parades around with that other woman, giving no thought to his poor wife. And everyone talks so mean because she has not produced an heir. You have always wanted to help hurting people, yes you have. Just like your mother, God rest her soul." Svetlana made the sign of the cross.

"I do wonder if she feels as much an outsider as I did in my time at court. Or perhaps I am wrong. She is the wife of the future tsar after all. Maybe she is just like the rest of them."

Svetlana picked up a medal and used her cloth to polish an imaginary spot. "I am surprised you are not more excited. Are the balls not as beautiful as you always dreamed they would be?"

"They are, yes. However, I am beginning to prefer the quieter life of our country estate. I believe that my change in preferences has less to do with the beauty of the balls and more to do with the backbiting and intrigues that follow the courtiers around like a bad smell."

Svetlana wrinkled her nose. "Bad smell, yes, yes." She returned the medal to its velvet-lined box. "Still, it is so romantic that the count introduces you as 'my new bride, the most beautiful woman in all of St. Petersburg.'" Svetlana sighed dreamily and sank onto the bed. "Most women would put up with quite a lot of smelly courtiers for a husband like that."

"You are correct, and I know I sound ungrateful about court and I do not mean it that way. I suppose my husband's introduction is romantic, but it's also so clearly untrue that it's embarrassing."

Svetlana stood up and put her hand to Alyona's cheek. "But it is true, it is."

"You feel that way because you see me with your heart and not your eyes."

"And so does the count."

Did he? Alyona had grown to hope so, but six months after their arranged marriage, she remained uneasy about the depth of his affection.

She quirked her eyebrow. "Since he follows up 'the most beautiful woman in St. Petersburg' with 'save for the empress herself' when the empress happens to be in attendance, I find myself doubting the sincerity of any of it."

"Pssf." Svetlana waved her hand dismissively. "He has to add that part because she is the empress, and everyone knows how jealous she is. There's no need to say the part about you unless he means it."

No need except perhaps for the fact that the empress had been the one to arrange their marriage. That, one could argue, presented a compelling need.

Alyona leaned forward and whispered, "I have heard it said that the groomsmen and valets at Peterhof are the most handsome in the country."

Svetlana's cheeks turned red. "I am happy to investigate the truth of that rumor. Yes, yes." She scrunched her shoulders up to her ears in excitement. "I have heard all about the fountains there—cascading steps, sculptures covered in gold, tile and marble galore. They say some of them are joke fountains too, they begin spraying if you are unlucky enough to step on the wrong rock or sit on the wrong bench. Can you imagine such a thing?"

"Joke fountains in the palace gardens with all the courtiers dressed in their finest? Do you really think that is true?" The Russian court was full of tales, many of them less factual than one might hope.

"I do, yes, yes. The maids at the Winter Palace told me all about them." Svetlana stopped and drew a breath. When she spoke again, her words came out slowly. "Of course, some of those maids weren't very nice." Her eyes narrowed. "Maybe they were just teasing me to see if I would believe them. Yes, maybe." She shook her head. "Maybe they were."

Alyona used her most upbeat voice. "We shall find out for ourselves soon, shall we not? At the palace?"

"The palace, yes." Svetlana's face brightened. Only two years younger than Alyona, her small stature, huge blue eyes, and cherubic countenance imparted such an innocent pixie look that she appeared to be no more than twelve. "Yes. We will find out. About the handsome groomsmen and valets, too."

"Yes indeed."

"How are preparations coming along?" Lev entered the room, carrying an open letter.

"Perfect. We shall be ready for an early departure tomorrow, just as planned." Alyona nodded toward his hand. "I did not notice the courier arrive. What mail did we receive?"

"A letter from Pierre. He arrived at Peterhof last night. He reports they are expecting a great crowd of people, with much fuss being made over every detail." He gazed at Alyona with something like sympathy in his eyes. "He does tell of a new decree by the empress. No young woman will be allowed near the grand duchess if she has not borne children."

"What?" Alyona put her hand over her stomach. "Why would she enact such a requirement?"

"She believes that excessive contact with barren women may be contributing to the eight years Her Highness has gone without conceiving a royal heir."

Svetlana snorted. "Somebody needs to explain to the empress what it is that causes a woman to become pregnant." She snorted again but quickly stopped when she saw the censure on Lev's face.

He stared so long and so hard that Svetlana went purple from embarrassment. "You are not a horse, this is not a barn, stop making that sound at once." He turned toward Alyona. "Perhaps it is time for the two of you to spend a bit less time together as well. We shall learn a lesson from the empress and apply it to our own situation."

Once when she was young, Alyona walked up behind one of her father's war horses. The resulting kick had sent her flying through the air and broken two of her ribs. Her husband's words hurt far more than those hooves. "Lev, please—"

He held up his hand for silence. "Enough talk. It is bad enough that the entire court will be speculating about why you have not yet conceived. Now, as something to add to the fodder, they will see us both shunned." He turned on his heel and clomped back down the stairs.

"Whew. The count sure knows how to make an elephant out of a fly." Svetlana released an exaggerated shiver. "Your 'own situation'? Pssf. You have only been wed six months. That is not enough time to have borne a child and would hardly count you as barren." She grinned at Alyona. "Even if you weren't with child."

"With child? What makes you think such a thing?" Alyona had guarded this secret and planned the exact moment in tomorrow's journey when she would tell her husband the news. When they stopped to change horses and take brief refreshment at Starorusskaya Daroga, the sun would be glittering off the lake and Lev would undoubtedly suggest a walk around it. She could already feel his hands on her waist as he picked her up to swing her around, hear the laughter in his voice, see the smile that would light up his entire face.

"I am the one in charge of your laundry, am I not? Certainly I have noticed that you have not had your courses for two months now."

"Oh, right. I wanted Lev to be the first to know. I am planning to tell him in the midst of our journey tomorrow."

"Then I shall keep my tongue behind my teeth, just as I have done for these past two months. Perhaps, though, you should tell him now and restore his good mood. It's a shame to see it all evaporate so quickly. He will be vinegary for the rest of the day, which does no one in this house any favors."

This was true. Once rankled, Lev became ill-humored and irascible for days at a time.

"I suppose you are correct. I shall go and tell him right away."

Alyona made her way down the stairs and stood outside the carved oak door of her husband's study. What to say? How to approach him? She took a deep breath, then pushed the door open at the same time she knocked.

Lev was standing at the window, staring out at the orchard just coming into color after the long winter. Pierre's letter lay open on the desk. As the two friends showed their mutual affection by teasing, there could be little doubt that this letter contained, along with the information of the new decree, some jab about Lev's manhood and inability to produce an heir. He glanced over his shoulder as she entered, then turned back to the window. "Go upstairs and continue your preparations. I have no wish to quarrel."

She made her way behind him and wrapped her arms around his waist, laying her head between his shoulder blades. "I did not come to quarrel, dearest."

"Alyona, I—"

"I am with child."

"What?" He spun around and took a step backward, looking her over as if searching for signs of her condition. "Is it true? Are you certain?"

She reached up to put her hand on his cheek. "I am certain. I had planned to tell you tomorrow when we stopped at Starorusskaya Daroga, but—"

"But my display of petulance forced you to change your plans." He pulled her into his arms. "Forgive me."

She leaned her cheek onto his chest, felt the thrum of his heart, and smiled. "Always."

CHAPTER 2

*A*lyona's back ached, but she felt so nice, curled up beside her husband, that she was loathe to move. When she could bear it no longer, she took care to climb out of bed just a small bit at a time so as not to awaken him. She grabbed her shawl and closed the door quietly behind her.

The distant clatter of pots and pans came from the kitchen below, where preparations were already underway for today's journey. She started toward the sounds, but the pain in her back had increased to an almost-unbearable level. Halfway down the stairs, it became apparent that this wasn't just back pain. It was something far worse.

Cramps.

Growing stronger by the second.

"No." She put her hand to her mouth. "Please, no."

"Is it safe for her to travel?" Lev paced around the kitchen, while Cook encouraged Alyona to take another bite of warm bread.

"Safe? Yes, it should be so. Comfortable? Likely not."

"I might as well be uncomfortable in the carriage as at this kitchen table. There is no reason to delay our trip further. There is nothing to be gained by it."

Lev put his hand on her shoulder. "You are so brave."

"I do not feel brave. I feel as though I have ruined everything."

Over two months of hopes and dreams had ended in less than an hour. Now, all that remained was continued cramping and bleeding.

Cook knelt beside her. "Enough of that talk. You have ruined nothing. It is common enough for a woman to lose a child this early on. By this time next year, you will be a mother and this will be only a sad memory."

Only a sad memory? Could this soul-crushing grief be reduced by so much? She knew it could not be so. Still, she determined to bear this pain without further burdening her husband or Cook, who loved her like a mother. "I am certain you are correct. Will you please send for Svetlana so she can help me dress?" She looked at Lev and offered a weak smile. "I am quite able to go now. Please, do not fuss over me any longer."

"Are you certain?" His tone held concern, but the pinched expression on his face noticeably relaxed.

"Quite." She pushed to standing. "As Cook says, these kinds of things are common enough. Let us move onward with our previous plans for the day."

Lev pulled at his beard and nodded slowly. "I will tell them to bring the carriage around." He hurried out of the room.

After he had gone, Cook said, "I know your heart is broken,

child. Mine is broken for you. I see what you are doing, putting on a brave face for your husband. Just know that I am here for you and will be praying for you every single day."

Alyona threw her arms around Cook. "That means more to me than you will ever know."

AFTER THE CARRIAGE HAD BEEN UNDERWAY FOR A few minutes, Lev yawned a bit too casually. "I think it best that we tell no one at Peterhof of this misfortune. Your deficiency might give the empress even more of an excuse to keep you away from the grand duchess. That, of course, has the potential for keeping us away from court, and we would not want that."

Deficiency? Oh dear Father, help me to bear this.

"Of course not, dearest. We must do what is necessary to retain our good standing with Her Majesty." Lev did not seem to notice how she choked on the words. She turned to stare out the window.

Small pink flowers had emerged through the recently thawed ground, stalks of barley rose from the plowed fields—everything signaled new life and the bountiful harvest to come. The carriage bumped on in silence.

Lev reached inside his coat pocket and withdrew his watch— gold case, cobalt-and-white-enameled dial, and a diamond-encrusted *E* at the center. It proclaimed to all who saw it that this had been a gift from the empress. He often drew it out in a crowd and studied it, as if trying to make out the time. As soon as someone said, "What a beautiful watch. Is that a gift from Her Majesty?" he would feign surprise, and with all outward humility offer it over to be inspected. Today, however, he shook his head, then snapped the lid shut. "We need to make haste. She will be displeased if we are late for dinner."

The journey progressed in silence, across roads still deeply rutted from winter's freeze. Alyona's back and legs ached. How she longed to get out and walk and stretch and have a few moments of relief. Lev withdrew the watch again and again, pulling at his beard and shaking his head.

A loud crack, followed by a sideways lurch, brought them to a halt. Lev flung open the door. "What is all this about?"

"The wheel, Your Excellency."

"Can you repair it?"

"It will take some time, but we have what we need on hand."

Alyona could have cried with relief. At last she could properly stretch. She climbed down, already feeling the easing of her joints. "I am going to walk just there." She pointed up the road. "Will you join me?"

Lev shook his head. "You go ahead. I will stay here and see to the repair."

Alyona nodded and picked her way along the smoothest parts of the road. She came to a stop beside a field, taking deep breaths of the fresh spring air. "Storms and shipwrecks. I will be thankful for what I have." It was a lesson she had learned from her mother—our plans do not always go as we had hoped, but God can make good come of them.

The abdominal cramping was easing. By this time next week, she supposed it would all be gone—any sign that her child had ever been here. She could not force herself to find a way to be thankful for that, no matter what she had been taught about storms and shipwrecks.

On a distant hill, far above the barley fields, there stood a single tree. Dark, empty branches, devoid of leaves or fruit or even a single bird, declared it long dead. What hardships had it battled all alone on that hill? Had that "shipwreck" been to the benefit of one single creature? Alyona could not see how.

Lev's voice shouted from below, "How much longer? It is imperative that we arrive at Peterhof before supper is served. You must work faster."

Alyona finally allowed herself to cry.

CHAPTER 3

This palace was smaller than the other royal residences Alyona had seen so far, and the yellow walls with white trim reminded her of her own home. She knew that the famous Peterhof Fountains were around back, but after a day of jostling and bleeding and cramping, all she wanted to see was her bed.

Lev pulled out his watch and shook his head. "We have certainly missed supper." He let out a long sigh but then turned to her and offered a weak but encouraging smile. "No matter. There are plenty more suppers yet to come, hm?"

The carriage door was opened by a palace footman. "Welcome, Your Excellency." He extended a hand to help Alyona out of the carriage, then held the door while Lev climbed out. "Shall I escort you to your chambers, or would you prefer to join the others in the green salon? Monsieur Boldachev has arrived from Moscow and is performing a concerto. I believe it has only just started."

"Escort us to the salon." Lev extended his elbow toward Alyona. "Her Majesty would be insulted if we were to arrive without extending our compliments."

Alyona stifled the urge to cry. Exhaustion washed over her, and grief pressed against her, but she placed her hand on his arm and took care to arrange her face in a pleasant expression. "I have heard of Monsieur Boldachev and his skill on the harp. What a wonderful way to end our day."

"Quite so."

"This way, please." The footman led them down a long corridor, through a set of double doors, into a room with a polished marble floor. Gilt tables lined the walls, each holding enormous jade vases overflowing with flowers. Green velvet chairs were aligned in rows, facing the rostrum.

Monsieur Boldachev was a surprisingly large man, with huge hands but the thin, delicate fingers of a young maiden. Alyona had come to dearly love the sound of a harp. It was one of her favorite discoveries from her time at court, so she determined to be grateful.

A bit light-headed, she looked toward the empty seats in the back row. How nice it would feel to sink into one of them. Lev, however, made no move to do so, as he would consider them beneath his station.

The front row stood empty. Reserved for the royal family and their special guests, Alyona took hope in the fact they were unoccupied. If the empress was not here, there was no reason to linger. Perhaps they could go to their chamber soon.

"You have arrived much later than expected." The empress's voice came from behind them. "Did you encounter trouble on the road?"

Alyona curtsied and Lev bowed low. "Nothing more than a broken wheel, Your Imperial Majesty."

"Hmm." She studied Alyona for a moment, staring pointedly at her waist. "I was hoping to hear news of an impending child by now."

The words knocked the breath from Alyona. Still, she

somehow managed to speak. "I was hoping for that as well, Your Majesty."

Elizabeth lifted an eyebrow, which made the glued-on beauty mark on her right forehead pull loose and stick out straight, like a fat splinter instead of a fake mole. "It is a shame, truly. I am certain that you will see this matter rectified as soon as possible."

The empress walked away then. She spoke to several people as she made her way up the center aisle—laughing, batting her eyes, tapping shoulders with her swan-skin fan.

Lev leaned close and whispered, "She will undoubtedly ask someone to move back so we may have seats closer to the front."

"That will be nice."

Elizabeth made her way to her seat on the front row and signaled two of her maids of honor to join her. She then turned her attention to the harpist.

Lev's face grew red. This lack of special treatment could only be blamed on one person. Alyona.

"It is a waste of time for a man to play a harp, do you not think? Men should be out fighting, or at least preparing for war. That is what men do, do you not agree?"

Alyona turned toward the familiar high-pitched German-accented voice. She curtsied while Lev bowed. "Your Imperial Highness, how nice to see you again."

"Yes, it has been too long, Alyona Arkadyevna, since I have had the pleasure of speaking with you. I was sorry when my aunt's matchmaking carried the consequence of sending you away from us. I am glad you are here so we have the opportunity to talk more about your father and his great courage. There is much to discuss." Grand Duke Peter turned to Lev. "This must be your new husband. What is your name?"

"Lev Petrovich Vorontsov, Your Highness."

"Ah yes, Elizaveta's cousin. You once helped my aunt, did

you not? Please, come sit with me up front and tell me all about your life when you used to be brave. And we can speak more about Alyona Arkadyevna's heroic father. It will be splendid."

The grand duke walked toward the front row, Lev and Alyona following. She could feel all eyes on them as they made their way up the middle aisle. Lev drew back his shoulders and walked forward with the swagger Alyona saw only at court. They were being invited to sit on the very first row by the heir to the throne, an honor that could not be overstated—or allowed to go unnoticed.

The grand duke sat across the aisle from the empress, pointing Lev to the seat beside him and Alyona next to Lev. She sank into the seat, thankful for the respite. The grand duke whispered to Lev about battles, and strategy, and war. Alyona attempted to feign interest in any of it, but found all of her concentration centered on keeping her eyes open. Over and over, the world blurred as her eyes crossed. It would be the height of insult if she were to fall asleep here. She pinched the inside of her wrist over and over again.

Finally, the concert ended. The grand duke turned to Lev. "Morning is still far away. Come back to my apartment, and we can talk more about the great battles."

Was she allowed in his apartment if she was forbidden to see the grand duchess? Alyona thrilled at the thought of meeting Catherine in spite of the empress's decree and her own exhaustion.

"I would love to, Your Imperial Highness. My wife, however, perhaps should go to our chambers and retire for the night. It has been a long journey and I am certain she needs to rest."

"Ah, Alyona Arkadyevna, we shall miss you, but yes, women are not strong like soldiers." He stood and beckoned Lev. "Come, Lev Petrovich, there is much to discuss."

The first rays of sunlight were shooting through the windows when Lev finally arrived at their suite, mumbling some unintelligible song under his breath. He stumbled into bed, the sharp scent of vodka strong on his breath. Within seconds, he was snoring.

Alyona had never felt more alone.

WOMEN WITHOUT CHILDREN WERE SERVED MEALS IN A different dining room from Grand Duchess Catherine and her maids of honor. Most of them were young and unmarried, and they chattered incessantly about finding a husband with a high position at court. Alyona pitied them.

Thankfully Lev had become somewhat of a favorite of the grand duke and was invited to dine with him each evening, thus sparing him the embarrassment of being, as he called it, "shunned" like Alyona. He'd arrive back to their rooms at dawn and sleep until noon.

One day, as they were preparing for luncheon, Lev straightened his coat and sighed. "I have come to understand that the rumors about him are true. There is not a whit of wisdom in that oversized head of his. Playing soldiers, that is all he thinks about. There is a set of wooden soldiers in his bedroom and another in his antechamber. Oh, you should see that one. The soldiers are carved of ivory, with jeweled eyes and solid-gold swords that can be removed from the miniature solid-gold sheaths." He shook his head as he straightened his epaulets.

"He sometimes even forces the ladies in waiting to pretend to be soldiers. I am thankful, for your sake, that you are not allowed in that wing of the palace."

The words, meant in kindness, pierced her to the marrow. "What is she like, the grand duchess? Does she play his war games, too?"

"In truth, I have hardly seen her. She has her own preferential members of the court. I believe they spend a great deal of time talking politics and philosophy in the British ambassador's suite of rooms. As dull as that sounds, I can see that might be preferable to the alternative."

How she wished she could join those conversations. What must it be like to discuss those weighty issues with the woman who would someday be the tsar's wife? A woman who was not satisfied with status and fine clothes but cared about the deeper things.

"Why do you not spend the afternoon with me, dearest? We could walk through the gardens, perhaps take a small boat out onto the gulf?"

He sighed and sat down. "Oh, that I could choose my own pleasures. Since our financial status is at Her Majesty's whim and she is growing older and often ill, it behooves us both for me to remain in the good graces of the heir to the throne."

Alyona started to remind him about the land the empress had sold him when they'd married. The land in the region was fertile, and their estate should be prosperous in the coming years. Her father's estate in Kazan had been far smaller, in poorer soil, and yet it produced a nice profit. Still, Lev liked to live in a much grander style. He had spoken to her before they married of having almost no money. She knew now that he truly was in a deep hole of debt accrued over many years. The generosity of the monarch would be necessary to climb out.

LATER THAT AFTERNOON THE CLOUDS GATHERED thick in the sky, casting a dreary pall across the grounds. The weather would keep most of the court inside so Alyona threw a shawl around her shoulders and went out.

The gardens were beautiful, and the fountains beyond belief, with golden statues generously placed all the way across the expansive grounds. At the forefront, the Grand Cascade fountain began just below the palace, made its way down seven green marble steps—each intricately carved with gilt images. It flowed past a golden sculpture of Samson surrounded by fountains, then down a long pool which ran the length of the gardens and eventually emptied into the Gulf of Finland below.

The Samson sculpture, her favorite, depicted the biblical story of Samson breaking the jaw of the lion. It was meant to symbolize Russia's victory over Sweden, but the story from the Bible was much more than Samson's defeat over the lion. It was God's strength, in a normal person, used in a mighty way.

She made her way through the gardens, noticing the green shoots and buds emerging from a long winter's sleep. A little white bench beside a stone pavement looked so inviting, she sank onto it with gratitude.

Suddenly water shot up in arches all around her. She jumped up and hurried away from the spray, but not before her hair, which formerly had ringlet curls close to her face, was now plastered against her cheeks. It took a moment for the truth to set in. Svetlana's joke fountains were indeed a reality. She would be thrilled to hear it—after she fixed the mess that was Alyona's hair.

She pulled out a long strand for examination and then burst out laughing. She laughed and laughed until her stomach ached and she was forced to double over. Still, she could not stop.

When she finally looked up, she noticed a trio of darkly clad servants making their way down the sidewalk, all staring at her as if she were crazy. She put her hands over her face. "I am so sorry. It's just the fountain…it caught me by surprise."

The trio consisted of a handsome man who was quite tall with a square jaw and an aristocratic air, an older man with a narrow face and long nose, and a young woman roughly Alyona's age who had a pointed chin and startling blue eyes. They were all wearing cloaks with hoods pulled over their heads. They glanced at each other, as if trying to decide what to do with this lady of unsound mind. Finally, the oldest man said, "I can still remember the first time I got caught by those fountains. I do not believe that I took it with quite the good humor that you have." Although he spoke in French, the language of the Russian court, his accent was unusual.

Alyona shrugged. "What else am I to do? Life is full enough of hard things. We may as well enjoy the things that aren't quite so hard."

"Spoken truly," the taller man said.

"I shall go in search of dry clothes and leave the three of you to enjoy your afternoon."

They nodded and headed down to the boat dock, while Alyona stopped to admire the Chess Mountain fountain. It looked like a series of chessboards descending from a slope, with multicolored sea creatures spewing water from the top.

When she turned to walk away, a small boat had pushed away from shore, carrying only two figures. Even though they had their hoods pulled down very low over their faces, it was obvious from their sizes that it was the woman and the younger man.

The other man walked back toward her, his expression sheepish. "I am supposed to be chaperoning, but I have a soft spot for young love."

"I suppose I do as well." She blew a kiss in the general direction of the gulf. "Go with love, dear ones."

"I could not have said it better myself." He bowed to Alyona. "I had best make haste before my crime is discovered." He made a show of doffing his hood as if it were a fine hat, then hurried around to a side entrance of the palace.

THEY GATHERED IN THE GRAND SALON AFTER SUPPER had finished, Lev still talking Prussian battles with the grand duke. Alyona walked to the windows overlooking the gardens. She heard movement beside her and turned to see an older man in a powdered wig, dressed in a European suit of blue silk. He looked familiar somehow.

The left side of his mouth quirked in an ironic smile. "You managed to get dry, I see."

It was the servant from the garden earlier today. "I...yes, I did."

"You are wondering why you saw me dressed as I was earlier."

"I confess, sir, that I am."

"I was acting in the service of a friend. More than that I cannot say. I would ask you, please, to keep anything or anyone you saw confidential."

"Of course. Your secret is safe with me."

He bowed. "I thank you. And forgive me, as I forgot to introduce myself. My name is Charles Hanbury-Williams."

"Alyona Arkadyevna Vorontsova. It is a pleasure to meet you."

Just then Lev came to stand beside her, putting a protective hand on her arm. "Come with me, my dear. There is someone I want you to meet."

"Of course." She nodded toward the man. "It was nice speaking with you."

"The pleasure was all mine."

As they walked away, Lev said, "Who was that?"

"Charles Hanbury-Williams."

"Sir Charles? The British ambassador?"

British ambassador? That explained his unusual accent, but it brought many more questions. "If he is, he did not say so."

"How is it that you came to be speaking with him?"

"He observed me getting doused by the fountains earlier today and was simply commenting that he was glad to see me dry."

"Hmm." Lev turned to glance over his shoulder. "I do not like his look. Stay away from him."

As they made their way toward a circle of courtiers, Alyona mused over what had just happened. Her husband gave every appearance of being jealous. If that was the case, then he must love her. All she needed to do was produce a child and all would be well.

CHAPTER 4

October 1754
One and a half years later…

*H*orses' hooves clacking, reins jingling, the creaking of the carriage as it lumbered along—these were the sounds that usually induced contentment. Today, Lev's silence drowned out the happier cacophony.

"We are fortunate the empress still bestows these kinds of invitations on us." Lev slapped the missive against his right palm. "Her patience is usually not this long."

"I am sorry," Alyona said softly. And she *was* sorry. She yearned for a child with such longing, she thought at times she might crumple into the emptiness.

When the courier arrived this morning, Lev had at first been jubilant. "They expect the grand duchess to give birth by day's end. We are to make haste to the summer palace in St. Petersburg to celebrate the blessed event."

Now, they sat in the silent carriage, air thick with tension, while Lev stared out the window. The bleakness of the landscape, after the harvest and before the snows, would do nothing to improve his mood. The silence dragged on and on.

"The grand duchess did not get pregnant right away, and now we are on our way to her delivery. Sometimes these things take more time than we would like."

"More time than we would like? It took the grand duchess nine years to conceive. That is not *more time than we would like*. It is absurd."

Absurd? Father, give me strength.

These were the last words spoken for the entirety of the two-and-a-half-hour journey.

THE GRAND DUCHESS WAS TO DELIVER IN THE smaller summer palace, on the banks of the Neva in St. Petersburg. The older wooden structure lacked the opulence and comfort of the renovated royal residences, but for reasons known only to her, the empress chose this as the place for the royal birth. Alyona made her way inside, thankful to be free of the walled-in tension of the carriage.

The grand salon's tables were laden with ice sculptures of bears, lions, swans, and peacocks, bowls full of fruit, and malachite vases filled with fresh flowers. Finely dressed waiters wove their way through the crowds carrying platters of fruit, cheese, bread, caviar, and imported French champagne. Empress Elizabeth was not to be seen. It was reported that she refused to leave the side of the grand duchess for even a moment, for fear the child would be born in her absence.

Pierre made his way across the room. His clothes were rumpled, and the smell of alcohol that wafted from him left little doubt about why his eyes were so red. "Countess, you are more beautiful than ever." He took Alyona's hand and kissed it. "Apologies to you that you are forever stuck with this bore." He grabbed Lev and hugged him, then stood back in mock assessment. "You, however, look dreadful—as tame as a shriveled, old matron." Pierre wagged his head in mock sadness. "Something must be done about this. Come, have a drink, throw some dice. You will feel better if you do."

"Lead the way, my friend." Lev bestowed the kind of warm smile that Alyona had not seen in weeks.

"Apologies, Countess, for stealing your husband. I believe, however, that you will be quite better off without this stodgy, old thing."

Alyona managed a smile and a nod, and exhaled a sigh of relief after the men had departed. "Countess Vorontsova, how good to see you. How is life in Taitsy?" "Tell us all about your estate." "How many children do you have?" Alyona threaded her way carefully through the usual conversations. As soon as she was able, she escaped outside to walk in the Summer Garden.

Even though fall had set in, hearty flowers were still blooming. She walked past the sculptures and fountains. *God, why will You not help me?*

She thought of Cook's words, when she'd found her crying over yet another month of failing to conceive. "Dearest one, He has not abandoned you. Just as He did not abandon your mother when she wanted another child. She was desperate to give you brothers and sisters, but it never happened."

"Really?" Alyona had sniffed and wiped her eyes. "I always wondered, but I never knew that. How did she handle it so well? Of course, Mamochka handled everything well, I suppose."

"She claimed the words from the beloved Psalm. *Even though I walk through the valley of the shadow of death, I will fear no evil because You are with me.* She shortened it to *Even though...I will...because You* and repeated those words over and over when the doubt tried to overtake her. She said that was all she needed to know."

Now, as Alyona stopped to observe the Neva, she thought of those words again. *Even though...I will...because You.* Soon the river would be frozen solid, but for today, it could still go somewhere, do something. During the winter, it would be locked in place, caught at the whim of the spring thaws. But not today.

When she made her way back into the palace, the room buzzed with whispers and excitement. Alyona saw Vanya across the room. She moved to join her friend from her time amongst the maids of honor. "Has the child been born?"

"Not yet, but they say within the hour."

"That is wonderful news." Alyona reached out and took Vanya's hand. "You look so well. Marriage obviously agrees with you."

"Very much so. My son, however, chooses not to sleep at night, and he seems intent on making certain everyone in the household remains awake with him." She shrugged. "I hope that a headstrong baby does not portend to an equally headstrong young man, or I do not know how I will survive it all."

A maid of honor, whose name Alyona could not remember, came to stand beside Vanya. She leaned forward and whispered, "Have you heard the news? One of the servants just delivered a stillborn son." She lowered her voice even more. "It is a bad omen." She made a show of crossing herself. "They say the empress will be quite undone if she finds out."

Stillborn? Alyona hadn't even considered that possibility. Her heart cried out for the poor woman and the great loss she had just suffered. What if it happened to Grand Duchess Catherine, too? After waiting nine years...if she lost her child at the end of her confinement, how would she bear it? No doubt the court would slander her all the more, making it so much worse.

Alyona found a quiet corner, and in spite of the lack of candles and icons, she prayed for the grand duchess. "God please give her a healthy child."

A hush fell upon the room. Alyona turned to see that one of

the empress's ministers had entered. No one moved, or even seemed to breathe, as they waited for him to speak. He surveyed the scene, taking his time to scan from wall to wall, before he cleared his throat and announced, "Her Imperial Majesty is pleased to announce the birth of a healthy baby boy."

The room erupted in cheers. Alyona's heart erupted in thanks.

Waiters carrying crystal goblets on gold trays swarmed into the room and delivered their wares to the attendees. "To the Romanovs." "To our great Empress Elizabeth." "To the new heir." Glasses clinked, tray after tray after tray was emptied, and the room grew more boisterous. "Here's hoping it won't take the grand duchess so long next time."

Alyona began to suffocate beneath the heat, the noise, and the weight of the increasingly vulgar toasts about barren women. She rushed to the door, longing for the freedom of the garden. Instead, she saw a deluge of rain, effectively blocking her plans for escape.

She noticed a hallway to the east wing and decided to follow it. The imperial quarters were in the west wing, so she should be able to wander about in relative peace here.

She climbed a set of stairs, stopping to appreciate each and every painting along the way. One in particular, a fishing vessel with clear sailing to the left and a squall to the right, drew her attention. The contrast was done in such a poignant way it took her breath. A storm on one side, sunny seas on the other. Which way would the ship take? Did it even have a choice?

Even though…I will…because You.

"Help me, please." A faint voice came from an opened door at the top of the stairs. Alyona walked toward it.

She made her way to the doorway and found a young woman lying on a mattress on the floor, wearing a bloodstained gown, her body drenched in sweat. Alyona rushed in. "You poor thing. Have they left you all alone?"

The young woman nodded. "They took my child away and left me here." She was shaking violently.

"Here, let me get you cleaned up."

"Water. Please, water."

"Of course." Alyona went to the side table, where there was a pitcher of water and a cup. She helped the woman to sit up and drink.

She gulped it down and fell back against the mattress. "More please."

Alyona poured another cup, then put the rest of the water into the basin. She found a cloth and used it to gently clean her. "Let's get you something else to wear." She opened a chest of drawers and saw several fine chemises folded there. Clearly, this was not the maid's room, and these could not be her clothes. Still, anyone thoughtless enough to leave her alone like this deserved to have one of her gowns soiled.

Alyona removed a plain white one and helped the woman put it over her head. She then lifted her onto the nearby bed. "I am sorry you have been so poorly attended." Alyona wiped the woman's face, pale and drawn, with startling blue eyes and a pointed chin. A flicker of recognition flowed through her.

"You...I saw you at Peterhof last year. In the garden, with Sir Charles?"

Her blue eyes grew wide at Alyona's words. How much abuse and neglect had she suffered? And at whose hands?

Alyona squeezed her shoulder. "Do not be afraid. I will not betray your secret. Tell me, what is your name?"

"My name is Sophie."

"Well, Sophie, I am pleased to make your acquaintance. I am Alyona."

"They have taken my son from me."

At least they had spared her the terrible news of her son's death before they abandoned her. Alyona wiped her face again. "I am sure they will return soon."

"No. They left hours ago."

Hours ago? Just the thought of it made Alyona ill. "Is this your first child?"

"Yes." Sophie twisted the sheets in her hand. "When will they bring him to me?"

"Soon, I am certain." Alyona adjusted the pillows behind her head. "I am wishing to have a child, but I have been married for two years and have not yet been so blessed."

"Your husband, does he blame you for this?"

Alyona did not want to speak ill of Lev, but a tear slipped down her cheek as she nodded.

Sophie squeezed her hand. "It is difficult, is it not? Everything is the woman's fault when it comes to having children—wrong time, wrong gender, wrong, wrong, wrong."

"Yes." Alyona choked on the word.

"They blame the grand duchess, too, for being so slow to conceive."

"I have heard that. I feel much sorrow for her. I am certain that she has wanted a child so desperately all this time." Alyona shook her head. "It is sad that people are so quick to pounce on the pain of others."

"Yes, it is. I am thankful that we have each other, even if just for this short time." Sophie reached up and squeezed her hand. "You should go before someone finds you here. It would likely mean trouble for both of us."

"I do not want to leave you alone."

"I will be fine now, thanks to your kindness."

"If you are certain."

"Yes."

"May I send a letter of inquiry in a few weeks, to confirm you are on the mend?"

Sophie's face brightened. "I would like that very much. Please send it to Sophie in the care of Nadia at the Winter Palace. She will know where to find me."

"I will do so. Now, I will go light a candle and pray for your quick return to full health, Sophie."

"Good-bye, Alyona. I shall never forget you or your kindness."

Alyona slipped out of the room and down the hallway. By the time she returned to the great hall, the celebration had grown downright raucous.

Alyona wanted to scream. At all of them.

"WHERE WERE YOU?" LEV'S WORDS SLURRED WITH hours of hard drinking as Alyona climbed into the carriage.

"I went for a walk."

Lev stumbled into the seat across from her. "You were not present when the empress came down to accept congratulations."

"I am sorry to have missed her." The lie tasted bitter in her mouth.

"It's a good thing for the grand duchess that she produced a male child. After forcing the court to wait nine years, she at least did not mess up that part."

He was drunk, and in a foul mood, but still Alyona could not stop her retort. "Forcing the court to wait? You make it sound as though she failed to conceive on purpose."

"Failed. Exactly. That is the correct word. Such wives might as well be sent to the convent. They are of no use to anybody."

His drunken rant was a repetition of the drunken rants of other guests repeated throughout the entirety of the day. She needed to steer his mind in another direction. It was the only way to calm him when he was like this. "Dearest, you've never told me the story of how you came to be in such favor with the empress."

"Have I not?" He crossed his arms across his chest. "It is a good story."

Alyona doubted she would like what she was about to hear. Perhaps this was the reason she had never before asked.

"I was there, you see. The night of the coup when she took her rightful place on the throne. In fact, I was first into Regent Anna's bedchamber. Once I gave the signal that it was safe, Elizabeth Petrovna sashayed into the room, already holding herself with such grace, such power. Meant to be the empress if ever anyone was. She made her entrance as if it were a state ball, drew back the drapes, and said to Anna Leopoldovna, 'Time to arise, Sister.'

"Elizabeth sent me to get the child, Ivan. He was fast asleep in the nursery in spite of the noise all around us. The little fellow had the heart of his great-uncle beating inside his chest, no doubt about it." Lev had always held Peter the Great in high esteem and would naturally impart some of that to his great-nephew.

"Was the child well-guarded?"

"Hmph. It should have been so. As it was, I entered to find his nurse cowering in the corner, holding a candlestick in her hand to defend herself, leaving the child alone and unprotected. You can never trust the lower classes. Self-preserving and cowardly to their very core." He made something like a laughing sound, then said, "I made certain she learned a lesson about such reckless disregard for her duty." His eyes grew bright with the memory of whatever he had done.

"I scooped up the sleeping child and hurried back to the bedchamber. Anna Leopoldovna reached out for her son, but Elizabeth shoved her cousin's arms away and reached for the child. 'Oh, come here my darling.' She smiled like the victor she was. The child awoke and began to cry. 'There, there, you come with me, your cousin Elizabeth. Everything's going to be all right.'"

A shiver ran up Alyona's spine.

"When we reached the carriages, Anna Leopoldovna was frenzied, pleading for her son to be given to her." Lev rolled his head in a circle then stretched his arms overhead. "Oh, how that woman could screech. It was inhuman, really." He rubbed his hands across his bloodshot eyes and yawned. "The infant Ivan, hearing this hysteria, began to wail with a force he clearly inherited from his mother.

"Elizabeth handed the boy to me so she could climb into her carriage. The moment he entered my arms he quieted. She turned, 'He likes you. You are to ride in the carriage with me.' Then she gestured at Anna and said, 'Put them as far away as possible. I cannot bear the sound of screeching for even one more second.'

"Ivan rode quietly in my arms, playing with the buttons on my jacket, cooing and laughing. The empress took him back after a few moments. Once again, he began to cry. 'The poor baby. The poor baby.' She hugged the child to herself and said it over and over as we drove toward the Riga fortress of Dünamünde. Finally, she handed the child back to me, and he slept soundly in my arms for many hours. The child was taken from me again only when the empress handed him to the officer who was to become his jailer."

Alyona knew of Ivan's fate, but hearing the story like this... It felt so much more awful than she had even imagined. A fourteen-month-old baby sentenced to a lifetime of solitary confinement so he could never take his rightful place as tsar.

Lev stretched his legs and laid his head against the side of the carriage. He let out a great yawn. "The next year, I learned of a conspiracy to rescue the child and restore the monarchy to him." He grinned at some memory. "That Lopukhina woman and her cohorts thought they were so crafty, but I rushed to the empress with the news." He closed his eyes, and just when Alyona thought he had fallen asleep, he said, "Within hours the effort was thwarted."

"Lopukhina?" Alyona's blood curdled at the name, remembering the stories of a woman who had been arrested on rumors, convicted after torture, then sent to Siberia after being publicly whipped and her tongue torn out. "You were part of that?"

His only answer came in the form of loud snores, with breath that reeked of stale vodka. Alyona had plenty of time to look at him, think about all she had seen and heard this day. An imprisoned infant and a brutally disfigured woman. Why would anyone choose to earn esteem at such a cost?

Somewhere during that long carriage ride, she could never be certain of the exact moment, she came to a decision. From now on, she would do what she knew to be right, whether or not it garnered the displeasure of the empress. Or Lev.

Even though...I will...because You.

CHAPTER 5

Dearest Alyona,
Thank you for your letter of inquiry. I am much recovered thanks
to your kindness. If only my heart could heal so easily from the loss
of my son.
Yours,
Sophie

Dearest Sophie,
I do not pretend to understand the depths of your loss. I pray daily
that our Lord will ease your pain.
Yours,
Alyona

Dearest Alyona,
Have you heard about the latest construction debacle at the
Winter Palace? Monsieur Rastrelli has decided that the old struc-
ture must be completely torn down. Nothing is to be spared.

Everyone is in an uproar. Honestly, such stuff and nonsense. I do not know if I should laugh or cry.
Tell me, what was your family like?
Yours,
Sophie

*A*lyona was relieved to see the spark of humor in Sophie's latest letter. She penned a quick reply, then watched as Lev and his entourage departed for his annual trip to the Urals.

Another lonely Christmas season was upon her.

A COUPLE OF WEEKS LATER, SVETLANA CAME UP FOR their usual morning routine. "I brought something that will brighten your day, I think, yes, yes." She handed Alyona a letter from Sophie.

"Indeed it will."

"I would like to meet your friend someday." Svetlana sighed. "Maybe when we next go to the Winter Palace, I will find her in the servants' hall."

"I hope so. I would very much like to verify that she is well. I worry about her."

"Yes, I will find her. But for today, I turn my attention to you. I am going to try that hairstyle like Baroness Gorbunova was wearing when she came to call last week. The one with the pinned rows of hair rolls, with frizzy curls all around the face. I think it will show off your copper highlights to nice effect."

Alyona's childhood friend, Roza, had come for a visit, while her husband was conducting business in the area. It had been so wonderful to see her, but her happy life as a settled mother and wife gave Alyona a pang of jealousy she tried to fight against. She *would* fight against. She was happy for her friend and would continue to be so. For now, she would read her letter and be grateful for the good things she did have.

Dearest Alyona,
Your mother refused to own serfs? She educated her servants? She
sounds much more sophisticated than most women who parade
around the palace like peacocks but cannot write their own names.
I am thankful that I, too, had access to a tutor.
Yours,
Sophie

Svetlana grabbed a comb, teased some of the light brown curls, then picked up a long strand of hair and rolled it around a large knitting needle, careful to work in some of the frizz she had just created. She pinned it in place, then sectioned off another piece.

"There really is no need for me to get all fixed like this. I do not expect callers."

Svetlana shrugged but continued her work. "Now is a good time for me to practice. If I mess up, no one will know about it. That is a good thing, yes, yes." Her fingers made quick work of the second roll. "Besides, the members of the household will see you. You are the mistress, after all."

The mistress? *I am the mistress!*

Alyona jumped to her feet, pulling the next section of hair right out of Svetlana's hand. "Beginning tomorrow, I will hold a weekly class for anyone who wants to learn to read and write."

"A reading class?" Svetlana's head bobbed up and down in agreement. "That will give you a reason to get dressed. Your mother, God rest her soul—" Svetlana crossed herself with the knitting needle still in her hand— "taught me when I was very young. The new people in this house will be glad to learn, I think. Yes."

"We will meet in the morning room at nine o'clock. Please spread the word downstairs."

"I will, I will." Svetlana stood unmoving for a moment. "That is settled now, so perhaps you could sit so I can finish?"

Dearest Sophie,
Your last note inspired me to begin teaching my own classes for
those in my household. I admit I fear I will not live up to my moth-
er's skill in this, but I am excited to do my best.
Yours,
Alyona

Alyona made her way into the morning room at eight forty-five, nervous yet excited. She set out a stack of slate tablets, thankful she had kept them as a memory of her mother. Hopefully she could bring credit to that memory.

She surveyed the room, which was lovely—blue floral-embroidered chairs, a polished plank floor with a pale cream-colored rug, and a blue-tiled Russian stove in the corner. It felt welcoming and homey. A painting of her childhood city, Kazan, filled one wall. It had been a wedding gift from Lev.

At nine o'clock, she walked over to the door and peered down the hallway. Where was everyone? She paced back across the room, straightened the tablets again, then made her way back to the door. A skittering movement caught her attention. "Hello? Is anyone there?"

A young housemaid peeked from around the corner. "It is me, Sonya Pavlovna, mistress."

"Good morning, Sonya. Are you here for the class?"

Sonya curtsied. "If it is allowed for someone like me."

"Of course, you are more than welcome. Is anyone else coming?"

"I do not believe so."

Why were more people not here? Did they see this as silly and frivolous? The thought formed a knot in Alyona's chest, but she willed herself to do her very best for Sonya.

"All right then. Let us get started. Do you know any letters?"

Sonya looked at the floor and shook her head. "No, mistress."

Alyona held out a slate pencil. "By the time you leave here today, you most certainly will."

Sonya lifted her eyes and a closed-mouth smile grew larger and larger across her face. "Bless you, mistress. When I told my mother about this, she was so proud to think I might learn to read and write, she cried all night." Her face turned pink, but she kept going. "I hope maybe to teach her a little when I get home. I just hope I can remember how to explain it all."

"What a lovely idea. Or, if you prefer, you may invite her to join us next week."

Sonya's eyes grew wide. "That would not be proper. She works on the Golovin farm."

The Golovin estate was just a few versts away. The family lived in Moscow most of the year, so Alyona had never been to the property. "Why would that not be proper? This time of year, surely they can spare her from her duties for an hour or two each week. I can send a note to the steward if that would be of benefit."

"You would help someone who does not work on your own estate?" Sonya's mouth fell open. She attempted to push back the profusion of frizzy black curls that fell across her face but was too bowed over to make progress until she finally realized it and sat up straight.

"Of course. I will teach anyone who wants to attend."

Sonya shook her head back and forth. "Maybe the lobsters will sing on the mountains after all."

Alyona smiled, then picked up her own slate pencil. "Today, we will learn letters and the accompanying sounds they make.'

"My oh my. Won't I be smart?"

The next morning, Alyona made her way downstairs and found Sonya dusting in the parlor. As soon as she saw Alyona, she hurried over to her and curtsied. She leaned forward, sending a cascade of curls across her face, and whispered, "Might my little sister come to class as well?"

"Of course. She would be welcome."

"And her friend?"

The next week, the class had five students.

The third week, fifteen.

JANUARY'S SNOW BLEW COLD AND EXTRA DEEP THIS year. A letter arrived from Lev.

Detained on business. Should be home by the end of the month.

"It is the weather, my dear. Of course he will be delayed." Cook knew her well enough to see the fear, although Alyona had been careful not to voice it.

"Yes, of course, it is the weather." Once Lev had the son he wanted, he would spend more time at home, she was certain of it. "Cook, what if I never have a child? Everything will be ruined. That was the only reason this marriage was arranged. As it is, I am already a failure in the empress's eyes. And my husband's."

"Child, you need to quit worrying about the opinions of others for reasons you can't change."

"Why will God not give me a child? I don't understand."

"It's not your place to understand. Remember the great Psalm? It does not say that because God is with me, I will never walk through the valley. It says, *even though I walk…* In this life, you are going to walk through some things. The question is, are you going to stick with the *I will* part?"

"I will try, Cook. Yes, I will."

February turned to March.

Detained in Moscow on business.

March melted into April.

Needed in St. Petersburg.

"I AM SORRY I AM LATE TO CLASS, MISTRESS, BUT I found more onion peels and needed to get them to Cook right away." Sonya picked up her slate from the table and took a seat on the floor.

"Of course, Sonya. We need every available peel on this blessed week."

"Strange, is it not, that peels from yellow onions can dye a white eggshell red?" Sonya shook her head. "It does not make sense to me, but I am glad of it. Especially at Easter. You have said that you will teach us science in the future? Perhaps we can learn how this happens."

A chorus of agreement resounded through the room.

"Perhaps we shall add a bit of science to our studies soon." As inadequate as Alyona felt as she attempted to teach the assembled group, their enthusiasm gave her a feeling of worth and accomplishment that had long been lacking from her life.

"After Easter, when I finally get to taste Cook's kulich bread. I am told she makes the finest in all of the Russias." Sonya licked her lips.

"I believe that is probably true." Alyona's mouth watered thinking about the sweet bread with white icing that graced the traditional Easter meal.

"We shall all have our stomachs filled again—meat and cheese and eggs. I know the fast is for everyone, but I believe I must be the hungriest person in all of the Russias right now." Sonya put her hand on her stomach, then her face grew serious. "Except for those poor wretches working on the road." She crossed herself.

"Who are you speaking of?"

"The prisoners. Did you not know? They have moved a work camp just outside the city to help prepare the roads for travel after the melt. They look like a crew of skeletons." Several others nodded their agreement.

A memory passed through Alyona's mind of her mother, and with it came a new idea. "Everyone practice your letters, please. I shall return in a moment."

Alyona raced down the stairs and into the kitchen. "Cook. I have an idea, and I need your help."

ALYONA LEANED OVER THE LONG KITCHEN COUNTER, putting dollops of a beef-and-vegetable mixture on a row of cooked cabbage leaves. "I have never understood how you roll the golubtsy so neatly. Every time I try, the cabbage breaks apart and I am left with nothing but a pile of filling."

Cook made quick work rolling the leaves around the dollop she had just placed. "Nothing good comes without practice." She rolled up another and another.

"There you are. I have searched the house from top to bottom and had begun to despair."

Alyona swung around to see Lev at the kitchen door, a wry smile on his face. "Lev, dearest, you are home." She threw off her apron, rushed across the room, and wrapped her arms around him.

"That is a nice greeting for a man who's been out on the road for far too long." He picked her up to hug her. When he set her down, he cocked his head. "The two of you are planning to feed half of Russia, by the look of that platter. Are we expecting guests?"

"Not exactly." Alyona had not written Lev about her new projects. She supposed it would be better when he arrived home and saw it for himself.

He pulled away from her and looked her over. "What is that you are wearing?"

Alyona's cheeks grew warm as she glanced down at the old sarafan. "I was not expecting to see you today."

"Clearly." He grinned, but his eyes were narrowed as if trying to solve a puzzle. "Where are the nice dresses we had made for you in Moscow last year?"

Alyona shrugged. "I did not want to wear anything so lovely while I was cooking...or out visiting the prisoners."

"Cooking? Visiting prisoners?"

"Yes." She gestured toward the platter of golubtsy. "That is why we are making so much. I have been taking food to the local work camp on Wednesdays."

Lev's face grew red, and he worked his jaw from side to side. When he finally spoke, his voice was measured. "Am I to understand that food is being taken from my table and served to lawless vagrants? By my wife, no less?"

"Dearest, you should see the poor things. Half starved, beaten down. I felt as landowners, it was the least we could do."

"The least we could do? Because...we owe them somehow? Please explain to me how it is that we are supposed to give the things we have worked to earn to these lawless thugs, who would steal the very shirt off my back?"

"I confess that some of them probably would. But they are being punished for their crimes by the hard labor they are forced to do. Should they also be left to starve? While they are clearing off roads to make the passage in our fine carriages more comfortable? Please, dearest, it gives me something to do, a way to be helpful. When I was a child, my mother took food and medicine to the prison twice a week." She grasped his hands. "I have missed you so dreadfully these past few months. I needed to feel useful or I thought I might go mad."

His face softened and he reached out to touch her cheek. "Yes, I have left you alone for too long. I should not have done so." He looked down at his impeccable suit and swatted at an imaginary piece of dust. "Let me go clean up from my journey, and we shall have a conversation about what has been happening in my absence."

CHAPTER 6

"*P*ierre needs me to accompany him to Moscow." Lev studied the letter in his hand. "I fear he is frightfully inadequate at handling his own business."

Alyona wanted to remind him that he had only been home for a couple of weeks, but the glint of excitement in his eyes told her all she needed to know about his readiness to gad about the countryside with his friend. "Will you be gone long?"

"There is no telling about these things, but I believe it should be less than a month. I shall return in time for the harvest at the very latest."

The harvest was several months from now. "That seems so long."

He shrugged and pulled on his newly acquired boots, crafted of fine lambskin with jeweled buckles. He put his hand under her chin. "I am not cut out for long periods of time in a country manor. Pierre can help me expend some of my energy, and I shall be home in time for us to participate in the winter season in St. Petersburg." He leaned forward and kissed her quickly. "See to the running of the household in my absence. Be mindful not to waste our resources in ways that are not beneficial."

"Of course." She could not help but look at his boots—knowing they cost more than most of their servants made in a year—and her heart hurt at his definition of beneficial.

She waited until his departure before she made her way into the kitchen. "Cook, as you know, the count has asked me to take only leftovers from our table to the work camps on Wednesdays."

Cook sighed. "Yes."

"So would you please triple the luncheon and dinner order for Tuesdays?"

Cook peered at Alyona through narrowed eyes, then slowly nodded. "Yes, I can. I have long thought we were a bit short of food for our Tuesday meals."

"Exactly as I have believed. There need be no more said about it."

"Well done, mistress."

Alyona made her way out of the kitchen and went in search of Dmitri. She found the foreman in the largest storage barn, sorting out burlap bags full of seed. He stood when he saw her. "Good afternoon, Countess. Is there a way I can be of service to you?"

"I have been thinking about the occasional travelers who happen upon our land. Some of them come to the door to ask for assistance, some are ashamed to do so, requiring them to either leave hungry or further degrade themselves by taking what they need without permission."

"Stealing, you mean."

"Yes. But what if we plant a small garden simply for the benefit of sojourners? We could spread the word that everything in that garden is available for whoever might need it."

"The idea is noble, but what happens when a profiteer comes and takes the whole lot?"

"Then I will consider my experiment failed. But I would like to try it."

He nodded. "You have a kind heart, I will not deny that. I hope those you would help prove worthy of it."

"Thank you, Dmitri."

As she made it back to the door of the barn, he called, "Mistress? I was thinking to plant this garden somewhere that the count would not be bothered by the sight of it when next he returns home. On the edge of the far pasture, perhaps? And maybe it would be best not to worry him with talk of it, either. He might find it...distracting."

Alyona turned and smiled. "The count does have a lot on his mind. I believe your idea is a sound one."

He tipped his cap. "I will see it done."

Lonely months came and went. Alyona turned her hopes toward the winter social season for a chance to spend time with Lev and strengthen their marriage. However, due to demolition and renovation at the Winter Palace, smaller gatherings in smaller ballrooms were de rigueur, and the empress failed to add their names to the guest list of any of the imperial functions.

Although they attended many beautiful private balls, the lack of an imperial invitation kept Lev in a constant state of anger. "Your unwillingness to produce a child has caused me to partake in your shunning!"

How many times did she hear these words? Too many to count. When he left for his annual yuletide trip to the Ural Mountains, relief—and guilt at feeling relief—battled within Alyona in equal measure.

And then, the question became a hope, the hope became a certainty. Things were about to get better at last.

She thought carefully about the wording of the letter, and prayed that it would be received with joy and not pain.

Dearest Sophie,
I hesitate to write this, fearing that putting the words to paper
will render it all a dream. At last, though, I can confidently say
that it is not a dream. I am with child. My confinement should be
during the holy season of Easter. It is such an answer to a long
given prayer.
A

She would not send the letter until Lev returned from the Urals, because he must be the first to know aside from Svetlana and Cook, who had long ago guessed the truth due to Alyona's extreme morning sickness. Each day Alyona prayed that her husband would return. With these glad tidings, he would once again become the kind and patient man he had been at the beginning of their marriage.

In late January, an express messenger arrived with a letter. She took it with trembling hands.

There is to be a ball tomorrow night at the temporary Winter
Palace and the empress has invited us. I will meet you at the palace
gates at 6:00 p.m. Do not be late.

Tomorrow then. At last the time had come.

CHAPTER 7

*A*lyona's stomach bulged only a little, so Svetlana was able to make quick adjustments to one of her gowns. It was a deep-burgundy silk, embroidered with the same burgundy-colored ribbon and sewn with gold thread. Lace adorned the sleeves and neckline. "I am thankful this has never been worn to an imperial event, so it doesn't have the stamp on it."

Svetlana fluffed the lace on the sleeve. "I do not understand why the empress would want to put ink on ladies' fine gowns. No, I do not. Why must a lady wear a dress only once? Before you went to court, we thought the stories of imperial balls and the circulating servants with their ink to be a fiction." She shook her head sadly. "Such a waste, such a waste."

One of many wasteful things at the Imperial Court.

Lev nodded his approval when she arrived. "You are looking well. That dress suits you."

They made their way inside the room filled with candlelight and crystal and beautifully dressed women. The smell of perfume and shoe leather and freshly polished marble floors overwhelmed her, bringing with them the emotions of hope and despair and longing and rejection of the past few years. They crashed down upon her hard. Suddenly she was crying.

Cook had told her that pregnancy might play tricks with her emotions. Now, Alyona could not stop the tears from trickling down her cheeks, but she did at least manage to remain silent in her heaving sobs.

"What is wrong with you? You are embarrassing me. Stop that at once," Lev growled in something just above a whisper.

She dabbed at her eyes and turned away. The tears would not stop, in spite of his anger. She managed to make it to a window and pretend to be peering out so she could keep her back turned to prying eyes. Finally, she was able to quash the flow. As she dabbed her eyes one last time, knowing they were still red and puffy, a woman approached who seemed to be about Alyona's age. Maybe younger.

"Ah, there you are." She put her hand on Lev's arm and smiled up at him impishly before turning her attention and blatant appraisal to Alyona. She quirked an eyebrow. "So, you are the wife I have heard so much about." She did not let go of Lev's arm.

Lev at least had the decency to seem embarrassed. He gestured toward Alyona. "May I present my wife, Alyona Arkadyevna." Then he gestured toward the woman. "Oksana Alexandrovna."

The two women curtsied. "Pleased to meet you." Alyona said the words but was not at all certain they were true. Something about the way Oksana held on to her husband's arm and the way she examined Alyona from head to toe, let her know that this was not a woman who was looking for a friend.

"It's a pleasure to meet you, countess." Oksana was short, barely five feet tall. Slightly plump, with a large chest that the low and tight cut of her gown was obviously intended to showcase. She thrust her shoulders back a little and wiggled before looking up at Lev. "You never told me that your wife was so... tall. And bony. Do you not feed her?" She leaned toward Alyona as if about to share a confidence with a close friend. "My dear, you really need to pinch your cheeks a bit. I hate to say it, but you look dreadfully pale."

Alyona squared her shoulders and determined that she would be polite to this woman. After all, her own mother had been considered brash and uncouth by her father's circle of friends and family. She would not treat another woman the way her mother had been treated. "I thank you for letting me know." She reached up and pinched her cheeks. "I believe the journey from Taitsy must have taken more out of me than I realized."

"Oh, right, Taitsy. You have a darling little house there, correct? Lev Petrovich has told me all about it."

Why would her husband be telling this woman all about his home in Taitsy? "Yes, it is a lovely place."

"Hmm." She smiled again, then looked at Lev. "You simply must have your wife call at my house while she is in town." She turned her attention to Alyona. "I just bought a little place, down the way from the Winter Palace. Since I live alone, there is far too much space for me to make use of by myself, so I am always asking my friends to call. Anytime, anytime at all."

"Thank you." Alyona waited for Lev to say something about this. He remained silent.

A waiter came by with goblets of vodka, cherry brandy, and champagne. Alyona took champagne, but just the thought of it made her stomach queasy. Still, it would give her something to hold on to besides the fan, which currently dangled from her wrist. Oksana took two glasses of vodka, as did Lev.

They laughed, held their glasses out to each other, and then simultaneously polished off the first glass in one swig. "Ohh, that was nice." Oksana giggled. She held out her second glass, which Lev clinked with his own, and then they repeated the process. This time they both burst out laughing.

"See what you have been missing by hanging out in your little manor house? It is much more fun here in the city where festive things are happening." She waved at someone across the room. "Oh, there is Princess Anya. I simply must make certain she knows to stop by tomorrow." As she walked away, Oksana sauntered and shimmied in a way that drew more than a fair amount of attention—the disapproving sort by the women and the intrigued sort by many of the men.

Alyona felt eyes upon her and looked to see Prince Andrei across the room. A beautiful young woman she had never seen before stood gazing up at him, not bothering to hide the adoration in her eyes. His wife, Princess Maria, was on his other side, seemingly oblivious to it all. He nodded toward Alyona. She nodded back, then turned away, appalled at his obvious philandering and thankful that she had escaped becoming another of his conquests.

"You should be more like her." Lev pointed toward Oksana with the new glass of vodka he had just snatched from a passing waiter. "She is fun to be around. I never met your mother, but I always heard that she was fun. There must be a bit of her inside you somewhere."

"My mother never would have dressed like that." Brash perhaps, but her mother was not a tart.

Lev tossed back his vodka. "Perhaps not, but I doubt she would have stood at a window crying in the middle of a beautiful ball at the Winter Palace—even if it is a temporary one."

Had she been stifling to her husband? A bore? The probable truth of this hurt, and she determined to be more effervescent.

"Ah, there you are." The empress floated up behind them in a flowing gown of all silver. "Now, Alyona, your husband tells me that you have yet to produce the much-desired heir. When we had this problem with the grand duchess, we took to locking the two of them into their room at night. This took several years, I confess, but in the end it did prove effective. However, how are we to do that with the two of you if you refuse to even come to the city with your husband?"

Refuse? The idea was absurd, and the thought that Lev had been perpetuating this falsehood landed like a smack across the face. Alyona did the one thing she knew would shut this conversation down.

She curtsied deeply and said, "I thank Your Imperial Majesty for your concern. I can safely report, however, that it will not be necessary."

These words drew Lev's attention. "What do you mean?"

"I am with child. According to the midwife, my confinement should occur sometime around Easter."

"That is wonderful news." The empress signaled a waiter who brought over her cherry brandy, which Lev also accepted. Alyona still had a full glass of champagne in her hand.

"A toast. To the next generation of Count Vorontsov!"

Lev sipped, then set his drink aside and spun Alyona in the air. "You have made me very happy."

Later, when Oksana sauntered back over, he hardly seemed to notice her and rebuffed all her attempts to engage him in any way. It was just as Alyona had believed. A baby was going to solve all their problems.

She looked forward to the future with hope—things were going to get better now. Much better.

LEV RETURNED TO THE ESTATE WITH HER THE NEXT day. He rose early and set about working on the books and checking on the barns and storehouses, something he had hardly acknowledged in the past year.

A courier arrived from the palace, carrying a package for Alyona. She opened the box to find a beautiful sapphire brooch, with diamonds interspersed so they appeared to be the moon and stars in a night sky.

A gift for the mother to be. May it be the first of many.
Elizabeth Petrovna

"I WONDER IF SHE MEANS THE FIRST OF MANY children or the first of many gifts?" Lev turned the brooch over in his hands, admiring the fine workmanship. He put his hand on Alyona's cheek. "In either case, I agree with her completely." He leaned forward and kissed her gently.

CHAPTER 8

*A*lyona's energy increased with her expanding waistline, and Lev took fewer trips away. He still seemed restless, but he was making an obvious effort to contain it. This child, especially if it was a son, would finally help him settle in and become the man Alyona knew he could become. He truly had a good heart. It just needed a strong anchor.

As Lent approached and with just a month left before the baby's arrival, Lev sat beside her and took her hands in his. "I do not want you to participate in the fast this year."

"Not participate? This year more than any it is proper to be grateful and humble before God."

He stroked her hands with his thumbs and looked deep into her eyes. "I know you believe that. I have never asked you to change your convictions on my account, but for the sake of our baby...you need nourishment. Vegetables and water are not enough."

"Plenty of women—"

"Please," he reached out his right hand to cup her cheek, "at least promise me you will drink milk every day. Or what about fish? Fish is allowed on certain days, yes? What if you eat fish on more than the allotted days?"

"I…it wouldn't be right."

He dropped his hand, his face turning red. He stood and began to pace. His jaw moved side to side, as it did when he was trying to control his temper. "You know that I have never kept the fast, nor did your father, as you have told me. Yet are we both not men whom God has placed in your life for guidance?"

"My father did keep the Lenten fast, just not the Christmas one. Please try to understand. I must follow the convictions of my heart and my soul." As she stood, a searing pain tore across her abdomen. "Ahhh." She dropped back into the chair, feeling as if something inside her had ripped apart.

"What is it? Is the baby coming?" He knelt before her.

Something wet gushed between her legs. "Yes, I believe that it must be so."

"It is too early."

"I do not think the baby understands that." She tried to smile but doubled over in pain.

"I shall send for the midwife right away." Lev placed his hand on her back. "There, there. It will all be fine. Let's get you upstairs to the bed."

The pain lessened a bit. She managed to sit up and take his extended hand. As she stood, another ripping pain forced her back to the chair. Finally, she managed to stand again, and as she did, dark spots floated before her eyes, then cleared.

"What is…? That cannot be right…" Lev's voice trailed off.

Alyona turned to see the entire chair seat covered in blood. The room began to sway. "I am sorry." She felt herself falling forward and then the world went black.

Time passed—years, decades, centuries, God only knows—in a fog of pain and darkness and delirium. Alyona's mother hovered above her, stroked her forehead, and spoke words of comfort. Her father stood in the corner, hand on his saber.

And then she was alone in her room, curtains drawn tight, but the sliver of light around the edges declared it daytime. Her lips were stuck together and scratchy, her throat parched.

A water pitcher and cup stood on the table beside the bed. Slowly, she managed to sit up, although each movement was excruciating. She turned to dangle her feet over the edge of the bed, took a few deep breaths, then pushed herself to standing.

A wave of dizziness surged through her, but she held tight to the bed, then grabbed for the table. After she steadied herself, she grasped the handle of the pitcher but found she could not lift it, no matter how she tried. It was then that she noticed her arm. It looked like a bone with skin on it. The room began to spin as she collapsed back onto the bed.

"What have you been doing?" Svetlana's voice came from a great distance, and Alyona felt her feet and legs being lifted and placed on the bed. She opened her eyes to find Svetlana smoothing the covers over her.

"Svetlana?" Alyona held out her skeleton arm.

"Mistress. You're awake. Oh praise be to God. Praise be to

God." She walked over and pulled back the curtains to let in some light. "How are you feeling? What do you need?"

"Water."

"Yes, water." Svetlana grabbed the pitcher and poured some into a cup.

Alyona moved to sit up again, but Svetlana quickly set down the cup and rushed to her side. "Let me help you."

"I can do it." The words came out so feebly, they didn't even sound believable to her own ears.

"Of course you can, of course you can. Quite able." Even as Svetlana cooed her agreement, she put her hand on Alyona's back and helped lift her up, then adjusted pillows behind her to keep her upright.

"What happened?" Alyona brought the cup to her lips and felt relief the moment the water hit her tongue. A small sip led to a larger sip and then a full gulp. Her stomach seized. Somehow, she managed to hold on to the cup but lowered it to her lap to wait for the nausea to pass.

"You nearly died, that's what happened. You got so sick, and even the doctor could not stop your bleeding. We all thought we were going to lose you. The entire estate has been crazy with fear this whole time."

Bleeding. That's when the first of the memories flooded back. "My baby? Where is my baby?" Alyona placed her hands on her now-flat belly.

Svetlana burst into tears. "She did not survive."

"No. It cannot be true. It cannot." Alyona buried her face into her hands and wailed, each breath feeling as though her insides were being ripped apart.

The door crashed open. "What are you doing? Calm her." Alyona did not look toward her husband. She was afraid of what she might see there. She continued to cry, a soft pitiful sound.

The right side of the bed sank as Lev sat beside her. He pulled her into his arms, putting her face against his shoulder.

"Now, now. You must calm yourself. Getting hysterical is not going to change anything."

She did eventually relax against him. "I am sorry."

"Shh." He patted her back. "You need to rest so you can regain your strength." He turned his attention toward Svetlana. "See that she remains calm."

"Calm, yes."

He stroked Alyona's hair. "I shall return to check on you later."

After he left the room, Svetlana sat on the side of the bed with the cup. "Let's see if we can get some more water in you. Cook will bring some broth up soon."

CHAPTER 9

*I*t was several days before Alyona heard the details—the baby girl born blue and lifeless after long attempts to extract the child and save the hemorrhaging mother. Elizabeth Alyona Lvovna Vorontsova had been lain to rest in the prestigious Novodevichy Cemetery in St. Petersburg. Due to Lev's high esteem by the empress—likely increased by the fact he had named the child after her—the empress herself placed a wreath upon the grave.

As Alyona sat up in bed, trying her best to eat the kasha Svetlana had brought, Lev walked in. "And how are you feeling this morning?"

She attempted a smile, although she knew it must be a failed effort. "Much better. I shall be up and around in no time."

He looked at her, his lips twisted to the side in doubt. "There is no reason to rush these things. You need time to recover fully. The doctor will be here any moment, to make certain you are healing appropriately."

"A doctor? I do not need—"

"Of course you do. How are you going to carry another child unless we see that you are properly cared for?"

"Yes, of course you are right." Alyona was thankful that Lev was looking toward the future.

Dr. Mandelstam arrived within the hour. His rumpled clothes and bloodshot eyes declared him overworked and under-rested. Still, his countenance communicated a level of competence and compassion Alyona found comforting. He spent a lot of time poking, prodding, asking questions. When he finished, he pulled the covers to her neck and nodded toward Svetlana. "Tell the count he may come in now."

The second that Svetlana pulled on the door, Lev pushed his way in. He made straight for the doctor. "Well?"

"She will eventually regain her full strength. It will take many months, but she can recover."

"Thank goodness. What should we do to facilitate her healing?"

"She needs rest. And quiet." He nodded toward the window. "As she starts to regain her strength, short walks in the fresh air would be beneficial."

"Of course. We will see it done." Lev stuck out his hand. "Thank you, Doctor." He moved a little closer and spoke quietly, although Alyona could still hear him. "How long before it will be safe for her to carry another child?"

Alyona held her breath.

The doctor shook his head. "Her womb was badly damaged by the measures taken to spare her life. She will never again be able to conceive. I am sorry." He donned his hat and walked from the room.

Lev glanced from the retreating doctor to Alyona and then back again. He waited only a couple of seconds before running out the door. "Doctor, wait."

ONE MORNING AT THE BREAKFAST TABLE, LEV WAS reading through some correspondence, and Alyona attempted to force down just one more bite of kasha. Lev pushed back his chair but remained seated. "I am going to St. Petersburg for the day. There are some things I must look after, and I have been neglecting my business for too long now."

"Of course." With such sadness hanging over the estate, he surely felt suffocated. "Shall I hold dinner for you?"

"That is kind, my dear, but I shall likely be quite late. Tell Cook I will eat in the city."

Alyona determined to spend the day thinking of ways to make things better for him around here. Or… "Shall we plan to spend the summer in St. Petersburg? I know that you grow restless here. We could secure a lease for the summer."

His eyebrows lifted for a few seconds, then he shook his head. "You need to continue to rest and recover. Besides, there would be little to interest you this time of year. Most of the court has gone elsewhere for the summer—Elizabeth to the Catherine Palace, Grand Duke Peter and his court to Oranienbaum. You would be bored."

"You said yourself that I need rest, not entertainment. There are many lovely streets and gardens in St. Petersburg. I can take fresh air there when I am feeling up to it, and you could see your friends and handle your business."

He smiled his most placating smile. "Perhaps we shall see as the summer progresses." He stood, walked over, and leaned down to kiss her cheek. "We shall speak more of it after I return."

A wave of exhaustion washed over her, but she would not succumb to it until after he left. "Travel safe."

"Always." He smiled at her, then made for the door.

Lev did not return home again for a full month.

CHAPTER 10

"*A*nd what is this *business* that keeps him in St. Petersburg? You'd think he would be here during the growing season, making sure everything was running as it should be. The past two years have not seen strong harvests." Svetlana brushed Alyona's hair, as she stated concerns that Alyona would never give voice to.

"He has chosen otherwise and to discuss it accomplishes nothing. I am certain he is doing his best—" Before the last words even came out of her mouth, the idea had formed and solidified. "You know what? I will do it."

"Do what?"

"I am going to conduct a tour of all the neighboring estates and even the smaller farms. The ones that are obviously successful. I shall study their methods and employ them here."

Svetlana smiled. "There's a little of your old fire back. I am glad to see it, even though I fear you will not be up to that task until perhaps next season."

"Nonsense." Alyona waved dismissively. "Run down and tell the grooms to prepare the horses. I shall leave after breakfast."

"That would not be safe for you."

"Of course it would. I am perfectly fine to drive my little curricle without any assistance." Alyona was especially thankful for the two-seater Italian carriage Pierre had given her as a wedding gift. It had proven useful for visiting neighbors and the occasional summer outing. Now, it would provide her the means to survey the farms in the area without need of an escort. "My matched pair are so slow and tame they hardly qualify as horses. The fresh air will do me good, and I will return in time for lunch."

After some argument with Svetlana, Cook, and the grooms-men, Alyona prevailed. Thus started her daily habit of morning explorations of the countryside, then returning to share what she'd learned with Dmitri. Her second week into this routine, she rode alongside a thick barley field, already grown up well beyond her own. She climbed down and tied the horses loosely to a tree limb, then walked into the field, being careful where she stepped. She squatted down and rolled a stalk between her fingers. "What is your secret?"

"What do you think you are doing here?"

At the sound of the voice behind her, Alyona leapt to her feet. She turned to see a man who was maybe a year or two older than she. His dark hair framed his face in unruly curls. His large size made her suddenly aware of how foolish these outings might be. She took a step backwards. "I apologize. I was just looking at the barley."

"Looking at the barley?" he scoffed. "To what end?"

"I live just a few versts from here, and I have been doing a survey of the neighboring farms and estates, seeking ways that we can improve our productivity."

"*You* have been looking for ways to improve your productivity? Why is your foreman not doing this?"

Alyona pulled her shoulders back, stretching up to her full height. "He is needed on the estate. I, however, am not."

He snorted. "Drinking tea with your fine lady friends, isn't that what is required of you while your serfs break their backs?"

"I own no serfs and refuse to continue this conversation. I shall seek assistance elsewhere." She turned her back on him and started toward her curricle, holding her breath while listening for the sound of chasing footsteps. With much relief, she reached her carriage unaccosted.

"Wait, please. You being here and all in your fine clothes…it caused me to misjudge you. I apologize."

Alyona turned to him and shook her head. "It's no matter. I shall not trouble you any longer."

"Please. Let me show you around. I am the foreman you were seeking."

"You?"

"Foreman. Owner. Laborer. I do it all around here." He shrugged and gave an almost boyish smile. "Permit me to introduce myself. My name is Viktor Novikov. Come, let me show you the new methods I have employed in this field. It has increased our output rather significantly."

Several hours later, Alyona returned to Taitsy to find the household in an uproar over her late arrival. She shook her head. "Never mind that. I am fine as you can see. Now, where is Dmitri? I have much to tell him."

CHAPTER 11

I have found a home to let in St. Petersburg. The carriage will
arrive on Thursday to convey you here. I hope it need not be said,
but bring only court appropriate clothes.
Lev

$\mathcal{T}$he household staff came out to see Alyona off,
smiling and waving as if she were their only daughter
moving across the sea. Only Svetlana accompanied her, and as
usual her eyes were wide and her sentences long with anticipation of returning to St. Petersburg.

As they crossed the Neva and moved toward the city center,
Svetlana gave a little squeal. "Oh, the new home is near the
Winter Palace. I just knew it would be, knowing how the count
likes fine things."

The carriage pulled to a stop in front of a pale-green three-
story home. Less grand than its neighbors, yet still a fine house
by any standards.

A couple of servants emerged and began to gather the trunks
and belongings. One of the maids said, "The count is out, but he

bid you to get some rest this afternoon. You are to dine at Madame Tverskoya's this evening, and her dinner parties tend to run well into the next morning."

Alyona settled in her room, then took a nap because, in truth, the journey had worn her out. She hoped she would have the strength to make it through this evening, and in a way that pleased her husband. She would make a point to be lively.

When she awoke, she found that he still had not returned, so she summoned Svetlana to help her get ready. Lev arrived barely before time to depart, and greeted her with a kiss on the cheek. "I am glad to see you ready to go. Madame Tverskoya made me promise we would not be late."

"Madame Tverskoya? I do not believe I know her."

"She moved to St. Petersburg late last year after the death of her husband."

"Oh, the poor thing."

He pulled at his beard and chuckled. "I doubt that anyone has ever used those exact words to describe her." He studied himself in the mirror and adjusted one of the medals on his jacket. "She is friends with my cousin Elizaveta Vorontsova. I believe you have met her?"

Alyona had indeed met her. She was loud, uncouth, and having an affair with Grand Duke Peter for all the court to see. "Yes, although it has been several years since I've seen her."

"Much like her, Madame Tverskoya is quite a brand of fire."

Alyona promised herself that she would observe this Madame Tverskoya. Perhaps there truly were things she could learn from her.

A SERVANT, DRESSED IN LIVERY EVERY BIT AS FINE AS that worn at the Winter Palace, met them at the door of the grand mansion. He bowed, took their cloaks, and directed them toward the entry hall, brightly lit by chandeliers dripping crystals, candles in gold candlesticks, and gilt-trimmed ceilings. It was as if everything in this house had been selected because of its ability to scream, "Someone rich lives here." Alyona's stomach turned.

From the next room came the sound of laughter. One particular laugh, a woman's, rose above them all. Lev turned toward the sound, his eyes sparkling with amusement.

They made their way into the room, and Alyona recognized the woman immediately. "Oh, I have met her. She was at the last ball I attended at the Winter Palace." The memories of that night, the obviously flirting woman, the delight of both Lev and the empress when they were told Alyona was with child all ran through her mind.

"Was she?" Lev's tone was a bit too casual to be believed.

Just then, the woman in question made her way over to them. "At last." She focused her attention on Alyona. "Alyona Arkadyevna, how good of you to come to my little gathering. It's been far too long since I have seen you."

"Thank you, Oksana Alexandrovna, for the invitation." Alyona gestured at the opulent surroundings. "Your home is beautiful."

Oksana Alexandrovna Tverskoya made a dismissive gesture. "It is quaint. I am certain your country manor is much nicer."

While Alyona did agree that she would prefer her country house to this, she managed to reply, "Nothing remotely this elegant."

"Oh dear, you are too kind."

Another couple entered the room, and she said, "I must go greet my other guests. I look forward to speaking more with you later." Lev watched her go with a bit too much interest. When the boisterous laugh once again filled the air, a shiver ran down Alyona's spine.

Hours later, when late supper was served, Oksana saw to it that Alyona was seated beside her. "Oh, dearest girl, I was so sorry to learn of your misfortune. I remember that night we first met, and you were just glowing and we all knew that things were going to be so happy. How terrible it all turned out."

Alyona wanted to disappear under the table. What was this woman thinking, bringing up such a deeply personal conversation while surrounded by listening ears? "I thank you for your kind words." She paused for a moment then continued in a way she thought polite. "I offer you condolences as well. I understand that you had lost your husband not long before I met you."

Oksana gestured dismissively. "He was old." She took a bite of lamb and continued to speak with her mouth full. "Thankfully, he was obscenely rich, and I was his sole heir, so he served his purpose beautifully. But...the loss of a child... It is too awful to think about."

Served his purpose? Never in her life had Alyona witnessed this level of vulgarity. How did one even respond to such talk? The entire table watched her, waiting. Finally, she managed to croak out what she hoped to be an innocuous question. "How many children do you have?"

"None, yet." She put her hand on her stomach. "Perhaps that will change in the future."

"Are you planning to marry again?"

Oksana gave a little smirk. "Perhaps. Unfortunately, the man I want is otherwise engaged at present."

Lev, who had been listening to the entire conversation, leaned forward and glared at Oksana. "You mustn't speak of such things to my wife. She is far too innocent."

"Innocent, yes." Oksana grinned at her and nodded. "Indeed, she is." She leaned back in her chair, made a little shimmying movement, then turned in the other direction. She did not bother to speak with Alyona for the rest of the evening. Or Lev.

On the carriage ride home, Alyona asked, "What kind of woman is Madame Tverskoya? She seems rather wild."

Lev shrugged. "As I said before, she is high-spirited."

CHAPTER 12

*S*vetlana hummed and twirled as she helped Alyona get dressed.

"What has you so happy this morning?"

"Well, mistress, there is to be a dance tonight at the barracks. Several of the other maids are going, and they invited me to join them. Me. To a dance. Can you believe it?" She paused for a moment and her face turned pink. "Is it all right for me to go? I'll help you get ready for your own evening first, yes yes."

"Of course. I am glad to hear of you having some fun with people your own age."

"Me too." She clasped her hands in front of herself and twirled again.

Still puzzling over last night, Alyona thought of Oksana Tverskoya, the girl of perhaps twenty who was gloating over her old and dead rich husband. Just how deep did the depravity descend in this place? "Do be careful, though. There are far too many untrustworthy people in this city."

"I shall, oh I shall."

THE NEXT MORNING, SVETLANA WAS BESIDE HERSELF. "There were so many fine young men, and they looked so well in their uniforms, yes, yes. And one young officer, his name was Boris, well…" She sighed. "He was the best dancer and finest man of them all. And so, so, so very handsome."

Alyona was happy for her young maid, even as her husband slept until noon, then left the house with vague comments about having business to attend to.

Svetlana came into the small parlor after he had gone. "Might you want to take a walk in the Summer Garden? Boris has invited us to join him for a stroll, and I would love for you to meet him. Yes, I would."

Alyona summoned joy for her friend. "I should be delighted to meet him."

Boris was a large man with brown hair that didn't quite curl but wasn't quite straight. It gave him the appearance of having just risen from bed without the bother of a comb. He bowed most graciously. "Countess Vorontsova, it is a pleasure to meet you."

"And you as well, Boris." Alyona stopped to admire the various fountains and statues as they walked.

The last time she had been in this garden was the day Grand Duchess Catherine had given birth to her son. And poor Sophie had lost hers. These memories did little to improve her mood. After a second lap, she said, "I shall return to the house now. I do not want to overextend myself."

"Of course you should not," Boris said. "We shall escort you back."

"Oh no, that would not be necessary. You two stay here and enjoy the fine weather."

He shook his head. "I would never forgive myself for behaving in such an unmannerly way. My mother raised me to behave like a gentleman." Over the next weeks, those words proved true time and again. The young man was courteous and polite to a fault. Alyona was happy for this, because there was no mistaking the look that passed between Svetlana and him.

Lev, on the other hand, returned late, slept until midday, then departed on "business," which necessitated him going out alone. One day at luncheon, he walked in unkempt and bleary eyed. "I have just learned that the lease on this house is being cut short. We will have to vacate by tomorrow."

What a relief. At home he would have to curtail his activities. Alyona made a point of using a sympathetic tone when she spoke. "Oh well. I suppose it is past time that we check on the running of the estate."

He collapsed into a chair. "The estate I shall leave in Dmitri's capable hands. I will stay with Pierre and continue to conduct other business here in the city."

"We are transferring our things to Pierre's home?"

"Not we. Only I. His apartments are not a fit place for a lady. You must return to Taitsy."

This news did not surprise, or even terribly disappoint, Alyona. "As you wish."

The next morning, Svetlana sobbed as the carriage pulled away. She held tight to a small icon of Gabriel the archangel, delivering the blessed news to the Virgin Mary. "Boris gave me this to put in the prayer corner at home, to remind me to pray for him every day." She heaved a great breath. "And he promised to write." She spoke not another word for the entirety of the two-and-a-half-hour carriage ride.

Alyona sat quietly in her own grief. She was not blind. The unity in her marriage had been forever broken.

ALYONA THREW HERSELF INTO THE RUNNING OF THE estate. Dmitri had made changes based on her research, and the crops and animals were all thriving. By harvest, their previous yields had been doubled. "Next year, knowing what we know now, we will double this again," Dmitri stated with satisfaction, as they stored up provisions for the long winter.

Svetlana wrote letters to Boris every single day, sometimes twice a day. Delivery was sporadic, but she got at least three return letters per week, sometimes all at once. One day, she came to Alyona sobbing.

"What is it?"

Svetlana shook her head and extended the letter for Alyona to read.

My dearest Sveta,
I have just been told I am to relocate to an outpost near Kazan
within a few weeks. I know, my love, that this is far too great a
distance for us to continue to have any hope at a true relationship.
I am herewith releasing you to pursue happiness elsewhere, as it
shall likely be years before I am able to return to St. Petersburg.
With all my love,
Boris

ALYONA WRAPPED SVETLANA IN HER ARMS. "OH, Sveta, I am so sorry. I know that you love him so and he loves you too, or he wouldn't have acted in such a selfless manner."

Svetlana buried her face in Alyona's shoulder. "It doesn't feel like love. It feels like desertion. Yes."

Alyona continued to hold the weeping girl until her shoulder was drenched. Finally, Svetlana straightened and wiped her eyes and nose on the sleeve of her own dress. "I shall die old and alone. Best to accept it." She shuffled out the door into the hall before the sobs began anew.

THE NEXT MORNING, ALYONA HEARD COOK'S VOICE AS she made her way downstairs for breakfast. "Stop crying in front of the mistress. Do you not realize her heart is broken as well? Her husband has abandoned her, and she has no hope to find new love. Even if he chose to divorce her, which he will not, she would never be allowed to remarry in the church. All she has to look forward to is being alone. You can at least marry someone else."

"I do not want anyone but Boris. No, I do not."

"Not even a sniffle when she is around, do you understand?"

"Yes." Svetlana's voice was ragged. "I will try."

"See that you do."

Alyona made a point of stomping on the bottom step as if she had tripped. The voices in the kitchen stopped, and she took her seat for breakfast as if nothing had happened.

Minutes later, Svetlana set the breakfast before her, offered a pitiful attempt at a smile, and said in a falsely bright voice, "It is a beautiful day outside."

"Yes, it is."

"Enjoy your breakfast."

"Thank you, I am sure I shall." Alyona sat puzzling about how to let her maid know that it was okay to be sad around her, when a knock sounded at the door. Svetlana made her way from the kitchen to answer it.

Although the front door was not visible from the breakfast room, it was close enough to hear most of what was being said. Or, in this case, squealed. Alyona jumped up and rushed toward the door.

Once in the hallway, she could see Boris, dressed in his finest regimentals. "I cannot leave without you by my side. I do not have anything to offer you, but would you consider marrying me and accompanying me to my new post?"

"Oh, Boris." Svetlana threw her arms around him, and he drew her into an embrace.

Alyona turned to make her way back into the breakfast room when she heard Svetlana say, "But I could not possibly leave my mistress. I owe her everything."

At those words, Alyona spun on her heel, rushed back down the hallway, and said, "Oh yes, you can. Nothing would give me greater pleasure."

"No, mistress. I couldn't."

"You can and you will."

Within two weeks' time, they had a lovely wedding at the manor house, and Svetlana departed for her new life. Alyona truly was happy for her, although her absence left a hole that nothing else seemed to fill.

CHAPTER 13

*a*s the Nativity season began, Alyona had not seen Lev in several months. She assumed he had left for the Urals by now, and he would arrive here sometime after the new year, as usual.

On Christmas Eve night, she stayed home to welcome visitors, Cook at her side. "How thankful I am for your presence here."

"You are no doubt missing Svetlana tonight."

"I confess that I am. But I am thankful. Boris is a good man, and it is clear he loves her."

"Yes." Cook nodded. "A blessing you were denied."

"We all have our burdens, do we not? I know that you are missing Ilya."

Cook squeezed her hand. "I confess I am." Cook's husband of many years had died last winter. "I am thankful to be here with you, child. Ah the Lord has brought me to this place, just as certainly as He has brought you here. For what purpose, neither of us knows. I am contented, though, that He has placed us here together."

There was a knock on the door, and Alyona went with Cook

to greet the visitor. She could not have been more delighted when she saw the dark figure covered in snow. "Viktor, welcome. Come warm yourself by the stove."

Viktor looked from Alyona to Cook, whose eyes narrowed in suspicion. "Are you certain it is all right? I do not want to intrude."

"Of course you are not intruding. Tonight is the night to visit neighbors, is it not?"

"Let me take your coat and hat." Cook shook the snow off at the door before she hung the things on pegs near the tile stove, turning to look over her shoulder as she did so.

"Viktor, allow me to introduce Cook. Cook, this is our neighbor, Viktor Novikov. He is the one who gave me such sound advice on our crops this year."

"Ah yes. We have had a splendid year in the fields. And your wife...is she not with you?"

He glanced toward Alyona, his cheeks, already red from the cold, going a deep purple. "I am unmarried."

"I see." Cook led him to the sideboard, laden with food for guests. "Please, help yourself as it was your wisdom that helped us have such a good year. You certainly are entitled to the spoils." She glanced toward Alyona. "Of the produce."

Viktor fixed himself a small portion. "Please, what is your given name? I heard Countess Vorontsova refer to you as Cook, but I do not know your real name."

"Cook. Everyone calls me Cook."

Viktor glanced toward Alyona, a bemused expression on his face. She shrugged. "It is true. From the time I was a child, it is the only name I've ever heard her called."

"Other than from my children who called me Mamochka, it is the only name I've answered to in more years than you have been alive. Except from my beloved husband, but as he passed away last year, that name may not now pass the lips of anyone living."

"You must have loved him very much. I am sorry for your loss."

"Of course I loved him. I pledged to do so before God, as do all who make marriage vows."

Viktor shifted uneasily in his seat. There could be no pretending not to understand Cook's meaning. Alyona shot a warning glare in her direction, which Cook ignored.

When Viktor tasted the soup, his eyes grew wide and he dropped the spoon back into his bowl with a clank. "This is the most delicious rassolnik I have ever tasted."

Cook beamed. "I thank you. It is my mother's old recipe."

"Your mother was obviously also an excellent cook. Please tell me, what is the spice you have put in here that gives it such a rich flavor? I simply must know."

"Spices? What do you know of such things?"

"I taste the dill of the pickles, of course, and the nuttiness of the barley, but something in the beef makes it extra savory and I cannot name it." He cast the most charming grin at her. "I do most of my own cooking. Since my land is small, I cannot afford to pay much in the way of staff. There is a lady who comes to my house twice a week to help clean, and she does some cooking, but to be perfectly honest, her cooking is worse than my own. I only employ her because her husband is ill and she needs the work."

"You could just give her the money."

"She would not want to be seen as accepting charity."

Cook nodded and pulled up to sit beside him. "I can see that you are a man who understands the better things in life. I believe I may have misjudged you upon first entry. Please forgive me."

"Another few spoonfuls of this rassolnik, and I would forgive you anything."

An hour later, several of the servants and local landowners had also arrived. Viktor was welcomed into their midst, and easy conversation flowed all around. Alyona could not help wondering what might life have been like if she had married Viktor—would it be like this, spending pleasant evenings at home with friends?

Almost as soon as she had the thought, she dismissed it. She had done what she had to do. Her actions made possible happy conversations around the Christmas Eve visitation table, even without a loving husband to share it.

By the time Viktor picked up his coat and hat in preparation for departure, Cook led the demands that he return tomorrow for the Christmas feast, backed up by a chorus of all those present. He put on his coat, placed his hat just above his heart, and looked at Alyona. "I would not want to intrude on the countess's Christmas celebration."

"As I said before, you are no intrusion."

He bowed slightly and put on his hat. "Then I shall be honored."

CHAPTER 14

$\mathcal{C}$hristmas morning dawned cold and clear, the sun shining gold in a sapphire sky. Alyona followed her tradition, and before she commenced with the household celebrations, she set out in the troika, laden with piroshki, brined apples, and spice cookies.

The prisoners bowed their greetings, hands over their hearts. "God bless you, mistress." "You are an angel." "Happy Christmas." "Have a fine day, mistress." She heard the words over and over as she handed out the parcels. And it would be a fine day for her. If only...

It was a constant challenge not to question God, to be angry with Him, even though such a thought filled her with fear of swift retribution. Still the questions niggled at the back of her mind. *If I was willing to give up my hopes for love to save other people, shouldn't God at least give me a child to fill the empty place in my heart? Why would a good God withhold those things from me?*

To have these thoughts must constitute great blasphemy, and as much as she tried to repent of them, they were always there. *Why?* It was the word that did not want to go away no matter how she tried to get rid of it. When she returned home, she went immediately to her icon corner, fell to her knees, and prayed that God would forgive her for such sinful thoughts. Again.

Even though...I will...because You.

Several hours later, the feast was in full swing. The smaller children were eating in the servants' hall, but the adults were all seated at the dining room table, laughing over stories from their youth. Viktor told of his grandmother's churchkhela. "She was a native of Georgia, and oh, that woman could cook. The scent of her simmering grapes filled the air so thick, just the memory of it makes my mouth water still." He made a show of licking his lips. "She would string her walnuts down an extra-short thread —many short pieces of candy caused fewer fights than just a few long ones.

"Her grape tartar was the best in all the land. We would watch her dip the walnut strands in the steaming mixture and hang them to harden, already elbowing each other for position to get the first one.

"One year, I convinced my sisters to play horse. They loved to ride on my back while I pretended to try to buck them off. After a while, I told them the horse must be fed. Somehow—" he cast a sheepish grin toward Alyona— "I convinced them to pretend their churchkhela strands were carrots."

"You didn't." Cook put her hand over her heart.

"Sadly, I did. In memory, I feel guilty about it. But on that day...*ne-eigh*." He lifted his hands in pretense of a rearing stallion. "I was the happiest horse in all of the Russias."

The entire table erupted in laughter. Alyona thought back to Lev's remonstrances that she needed to be more "lively." Well, these people were plenty lively, and they didn't require great excess to be so. If only he could see it.

"What is the meaning of this?" The thought still fresh in her mind, Lev's voice roared through the room. All of the servants shot out of their chairs.

"Dearest, you are home. We were not expecting you." Alyona tried to remain calm. One look at his expression told her this would not be a greeting of holiday welcome and cheer.

"Clearly you were not. Otherwise, there would not be a household of servants sitting at my table, eating my food."

Without a word, each person grabbed his or her own plate and filed out of the dining room. Alyona took a step toward her husband. "You have not been here, nor were we expecting you. It made no sense for the servants to eat in their hall and me to eat in here alone."

"It makes perfect sense." He glared at the retreating group. "Who are you?"

Viktor, who had his plate in hand, walked over. "Happy Christmas, Count Vorontsov. I am Viktor Novikov. I live just a few versts from here and am pleased to make your acquaintance." His manner and tone were just as polite as if they were meeting at a fine dinner.

"Why, exactly, would you be in my dining room? The rest of them work for me. You, however, can have only one reason to be here—to take what is mine—be that my food or my wife, I am not certain."

"Dearest, Viktor has been helping us learn more about the crops in this area. It is thanks to his sound advice that the manor produced so well this year."

"Am I to understand that the man who is sharing the Christmas feast with my wife has also been instructing my servants in better ways to farm my own land? This is outrageous." He walked over and put his face only an inch from Viktor's. "Get out of my house. If I ever see you anywhere near what is mine again, I will shoot you right between the eyes. Is this in any way unclear?"

"Not at all." Viktor carried his plate toward the kitchen, but Lev snatched it from his hands and smashed it on the floor.

"Out now, before I forget my determination to extend extra patience on this blessed day of Christmas."

Viktor looked at Alyona. His expression was so full of pity it made her want to cry. "I apologize for bringing a disruption to your Christmas celebration, Countess." He bowed slightly, then made his way outside.

Lev bellowed after the retreating servants. "Where is Dmitri?"

"He is spending the day at his own house. His daughter has been ill, Your Excellency."

Within minutes, Lev was galloping through the snow toward Dmitri's cottage.

Cook wrapped a protective arm around Alyona's shoulder. "Oh, child, I am so very sorry. Who knew he would decide to show up today? It has been years since he has returned home for the Christmas feast."

"Yes, far too many years."

ALYONA SENT EVERYONE TO THEIR OWN COTTAGES. She alone would be here to face Lev's wrath when he returned. She fumed, paced, and dreaded in equal measure. Finally, she went to the icon corner, dropped to her knees, and prayed, pouring out every bit of it before God. "Heavenly Father, as this is the day we celebrate the holy birth, please give me extra strength, so that I may be able to do Your will. Show me what that is. Bless all those who work on this estate. Soften my husband's heart. And if You will not..." Dare she pray what she really wanted? "I know what the midwife said, but with You all things are possible, are they not? Will You please give me a child?"

She stayed on her knees for a long time. Finally, the smell of smoke drew her attention, faint at first but growing stronger. She leaned toward the candle and sniffed but knew instinctively this was not the source. The tile stove against the far wall seemed fine, so she made her way to the kitchen. The smell grew stronger with each step.

That was when she saw it.

She ran out the back door, heedless of the fact that she was wearing no cloak and the snow was deep. Her husband stood with Dmitri beside a pile of burning barley. "What are you doing?"

Lev heaved another bundle on the fire. "I will not partake in the spoils gained by my wife's infidelity." He heaved another bundle and then another, all the while she was running around trying to fetch them and carry them back into the barn. "Stop, please stop."

He did not stop. Not until he threw the last bundle into the fire.

After he stomped back into the house, Dmitri stared at the smoldering remains. "He had me measure the exact amount of our harvest from last year. Everything above that he burned."

Alyona wrapped her arms around herself and doubled over in pain. "For the first time ever, we have been self-sustaining and profitable."

"Not anymore." Dmitri kicked at a pile of ash, sending it flying into the air. "Not anymore."

CHAPTER 15

Christmas 1762
Six years later…

As he had done repeatedly for the past six years, Lev returned home on Christmas Day. Alyona feigned naiveté at his motives and tried her best to make the day special. This year, after confirming there were not servants at his table, he brought reports of the empress's illness.

The day after Christmas, the post arrived. He scrubbed his hands across his face. "It is as I feared. Empress Elizabeth has died."

Alyona had heard rumors of dizzy spells and swelling legs, but by the time rumors reached Taitsy, they were scarcely to be believed. "Oh, I am sorry for her."

Lev scoffed. "Sorry for her, yes. What about us?"

"What do you mean?"

"Her patronage has been our support. Now that she is gone, our future is not so secure."

Alyona wanted to remind him that their estate was self-sustaining—and even profitable—now that he did not burn the excess. It was only his lavish spending in St. Petersburg that caused their current state of debt. "Your stipend was military in nature, correct? Surely of all people, the grand duke..." She corrected herself. "Tsar Peter will not take that from you, as soldiers and battles are his great love."

"That is all well and good, but he loves the Prussians and cannon fire. The service of a former officer who helped his aunt depose an infant tsar has long ceased to entertain."

"But he seems to hold you in high regard."

"True, but his wife does not, and she has great influence on the court. She may be our undoing."

Alyona wondered about the woman she had never met. What was she truly like? If she did cut off Lev's support, what choice would he have but to return to the manor, leaving all the parties and women behind?

At this point, she hardly knew what to hope for anymore.

LEV WROTE LETTER AFTER LETTER TO MAKE CERTAIN his position was secure. "I need to go to the city. I should be there while she lies in state, and for the funeral."

"Should I accompany you?"

He shook his head. "I will send for you when the time is right. Many factions are vying for power at court right now. It is not safe."

"You have said yourself that Tsar Peter has always liked me.'

Lev tilted his head to the side. "That is true." He stroked his beard. "However, there are others who also have his good opinion these days. As I said, I shall send for you when the time is right."

He departed two days later and the household sighed with

relief. His presence brought only tension and strife as everyone tiptoed around his temper. This thought must be a sin. Something Alyona would repent of...but later, after she enjoyed the peace of the morning.

IT WAS THREE MONTHS BEFORE SHE HEARD FROM HIM again.

> *I shall be arriving home in three days' time, along with Madame Tverskoya. The capital is in great unrest, and I fear for her safety here.*
>
> *Please make a room ready for her. She is used to a fine level of living. It would be an embarrassment if things are not as they should be. We will arrive before supper. I do not believe it necessary to state that there should be no servants or stray men sitting at my dining table when we arrive.*

Alyona threw the letter to the floor. She dropped into a chair, arms crossed, insides seething. How dare he speak to her in such a way? Finally, she climbed the stairs and made her way to the guest room at the end of the hall.

A lovely painting of the Neva hung on the far wall. Alyona reached out and pushed it into a tilt. Then she rumpled the yellow silk bedding, pulled a blanket off the small chair, tossed it onto the floor, and then pushed the chair over on its side. This act, though childish, gave her a moment of satisfaction. She opened the bureau drawers and left them all askew and kicked at the bearskin rug beside the bed, causing it to fold upon itself.

Her anger mostly spent, she found herself thankful that no one had witnessed her tantrum. She straightened the room, then reluctantly went in search of Cook. "He wants 'things to be as they should be.'"

"And when are they not?" Cook rolled her eyes. "I will see to it that the maids do an extra thorough cleaning on the back bedroom, the stove is lit, and the washbasin is made ready. Should I prepare an extra-fancy supper that day?"

"Yes, please." Although it irked her to agree to this.

"This Madame Tverskoya, have you met her? What is she like?"

"I have met her a few times. She is quite boisterous."

"Boisterous?"

"Some might call her raucous." *And flirtatious. And brazen.*

Cook nodded. "I see. Well, we shall prepare for her as best we can."

CHAPTER 16

Their finest plates and silver were cleaned and polished, Alyona was dressed in her nicest dress—a several-year-old emerald-green velvet with gold brocade trim—and the entire house smelled of herbs and lamb. She made one last round, making certain nothing was out of place, then pulled back the heavy drapes to search for signs of imminent arrival.

Nothing.

She repeated the process—through the house, checked with Cook, back to the window. Still nothing. Suppertime came and went, hours passed, and there was no word.

Well past midnight, Alyona gave the food to the servants and went to bed.

Long after she blew out her candle, she lay awake. What had happened? As the weather had been unseasonably warm this year, the roads were likely muddy, but that should not account for more than an hour or two of delays. Lev had spoken of unrest in the capital. Had they been detained? Attacked?

The next morning, she awoke to find Lev's side of the bed still empty, and the house quiet. She tiptoed down the hall, where the door to the guest bedroom remained open and the room unoccupied.

She hurried to get dressed and go downstairs. "Have we received any messages?"

Cook shook her head. "Nothing. Tikhon checked the roads this morning. He found nothing of any concern."

"Well, we will just have to assume they departed a day late for some reason. I suppose we should plan on supper and possibly luncheon with Lev and the madam."

Cook nodded. "Already planning for them. I shall have some refreshment if they should arrive in the between times, as well."

"Thank you, Cook."

Alyona spent the day in a restless sort of busyness. She straightened things that needed no straightening, adjusted things that needed no adjustment, smoothed down her dress many times. Today, as yesterday, she was wearing a pannier and a European-style dress, as much as she had grown to prefer the sarafan.

Once again, supper arrived and Lev was nowhere to be seen. Again, the grooms from the stable went out on a search but found nothing. Again, Alyona gave the servants the fine meal and ate none herself.

After four days, her worried imaginings could no longer be tolerated. She dressed in court attire although one of her older dresses. There was no reason to muss a good one. "Tikhon, I need you to go to St. Petersburg. See if you can locate the count or find out what has become of him."

The young groom nodded. "Do not worry, mistress, I will find him."

Within minutes, Tikhon came back into the house. "As I was preparing to leave, I saw a carriage coming up the road."

Alyona went to the window and observed a large carriage lumbering through the orchards. She smoothed down her skirt and went outside to greet them. Even from a distance, she could hear Oksana's laughter.

The carriage pulled to a stop in front of the house and Oksana climbed down, dressed in a bright-purple dress that shimmered in the sunlight. She sashayed over to Alyona, her skirt swishing around her with every step. "My, don't you look so quaint." She kissed her on both cheeks. "Such the country woman you have become, have you not?"

Lev followed, dressed in finery that Alyona had never before seen. Where did he get the funds for this? He had cut the expenses for the estate by a significant amount. There was hardly enough to maintain a standard of living, much less dress like the richest person in town. He made a show of staring at Alyona's dress and scowled. "Did I not tell you to be prepared for us?"

"You told me to be prepared for an arrival four days ago."

"I thought you could use the extra time to get yourself ready. Apparently, we didn't give you long enough."

Oksana swatted playfully at his arm. "That is not nice at all." She smiled coyly at him, then turned to Alyona. "Perhaps if we work together we can teach him some manners while I'm here."

Alyona could not bring herself to respond to this. She gestured toward the front door. "Please, do come inside."

As Oksana turned to make her way up the stairs, something about her made Alyona look a second time. Then she realized why.

Her fashionable dress, wide pannier, and clever lacing of the corset had hidden the truth at first glance. Now, however, there could be no denying the fact.

Oksana Tverskoya was pregnant.

OKSANA RESTED IN HER "CHARMING LITTLE ROOM" until suppertime. When she finally arrived in the parlor, Alyona searched for a topic of conversation. "Your hair looks lovely." It was the first thing that came to mind, but it was true. Alyona had never seen a more intricate style.

"Thank you." Oksana turned so Alyona could see the back. "I prefer not to wear a wig, so I would not rest until I located the most talented hairstylist in all of Russia. Thankfully, our former empress did not live long enough to steal her from me." Alyona gasped at this remark, but Oksana did not seem to notice. "That old cow pilfered my favorite dressmaker just last year."

Were there no limits to this woman's impropriety? Alyona frantically searched for a different subject. "How is your home in St. Petersburg?"

Oksana moaned. "It is so completely dull there right now, what with the time of mourning and all. Thankfully, the new tsar is much less ceremonial in these kinds of matters. His wife, though, has got to be the dullest person on the continent."

"I have heard she is highly intelligent."

Oksana shuddered. "She is so very tedious, arguing politics constantly. She is furious with her husband for calling back troops from the war against Prussia, blabbing on and on about how he has undone all the goodwill we have forged with our allies, blah, blah, blah. Then she jabbers for hours about philosophy, or European trade, or the rights of the serfs and peasants." She sighed dramatically. "Tsar Peter has his own obsessions, but at least his pretend battles prove entertaining. Thankfully his favorite, Elizaveta, is much more fun."

Alyona remembered Elizaveta. Her coarse manners made it understandable why Oksana would feel a kinship with her. "I find it hard to understand how the two of them can be so blatant about their relationship. In front of the entire court."

Oksana made a choking sound, which was clearly her attempt to stifle a giggle. "It's not like it will matter for long. Things are already in the works for the tsar to have Grand Duchess Catherine imprisoned in a convent. I expect it will happen by the end of the year, and then he will be free to marry Elizaveta and it will all be settled."

"He would send Catherine to a convent?"

"Yes. The church has issues about divorce, you know. A convent is really the only way to get her, or any other unwanted female, out of the imperial family. Otherwise, they are stuck, just like the rest of us." She cut her eyes toward Lev.

"But what of her son? Surely they would not deprive Catherine of raising her own son?"

Again, Oksana made the choking laugh. "Our dearly departed Empress Elizabeth rarely allowed Catherine to see him, as she wanted to raise the boy herself. Now that Elizabeth is gone, I am sure he will be left in the care of the governesses and tutors that have been with him from the beginning. He will hardly notice his mother has left the court."

Alyona thought she might be sick. "It is all so very heartless."

Oksana looked at her then, as if surprised. She leaned forward and stroked Alyona's forearm, as if petting a small child. "I have forgotten what Lev told me about how naive you are. I am sorry. I did not mean to shock you with the ways of the world."

"She will be shocked enough when our decreased allowance from the tsar begins to make a difference in our home affairs." Lev entered the room, dressed in a new jacket, covered in medals and gold braiding. "Hopefully he disposes of Catherine before she gets her wish to take it away altogether."

"She has always hated you, has she not?" Oksana made a dismissive gesture, then turned her attention back to Alyona. "That is why I told him it would be best for us to come here for a few weeks. Lev needs to stay out of Catherine's sight until she is locked away. Although she is out of the tsar's favor, she still has power at court. Elizaveta is a great friend of mine. Once things are settled, she will see that Count Vorontsov is taken care of, on my account."

On your account? Alyona was more than certain she did not want to hear her reason for that assumption. She gestured toward the door. "I believe our dinner is ready. Shall we?"

"Look at these darling little provincial plates." Oksana picked up the plate in question and turned it over. "Lev, I thought you were exaggerating about how plain life here really is." She looked at Alyona then with mock sympathy. "I cannot believe he would leave you in such primitive conditions. Perhaps the two of us can find ways to improve the household while I am here."

The plates, fine faience of blue and gold, had belonged to Alyona's mother—purchased by her father from an Italian craftsman. While they might not have been the fine porcelain used in the Winter Palace, they would certainly be considered extravagant for most Russians. Still, she forced herself to bite back the reply she wanted to give. "I would not want to trouble you in any way, but I thank you for your kind offer."

"It would be no trouble. Being this far outside the city, there is little else to entertain." She looked at Lev. "I have asked your husband to throw a grand party while I am here, but he keeps refusing me. Perhaps you could convince him."

"Since only a moment ago I learned that the income allotted for my household has decreased, I would not try to convince him to waste money in such a wanton way. Many depend on employment by this estate to feed their families. My conscience would not allow it."

Oksana turned toward Lev then, dipped her head with an ill-concealed grin, and peered out the top of her eyes at him. "My, my. I see now that I was wrong to underestimate the truth of your words. I shall not be so quick to do so again."

Oksana spent the rest of dinner prattling on about parties, and balls, and which royal or rich person she had met and who was her "great friend."

Alyona had never been so grateful for a night to end.

CHAPTER 17

*T*he next few days dragged on. Oksana was rude and overbearing most of the time—and openly flirting with Lev for all of it. Alyona retreated for long walks on the muddy paths, not having the heart to fight against it.

On the fourth morning, she announced her intention to visit the prisoners. Lev rolled his eyes. "If you feel as though you must see those crooks, I will not stop you. However, you will not be taking food from my house to them. They have made their life choices and are paying the penalty. I will not feed them from the bounty of my better choices."

"Is it quite safe for you to go there? It seems to me a woman should not be gadding about the countryside by herself. It is just asking for trouble." Oksana cut a sideways glance at Lev, then made little effort to hide her condescending grin.

"I thank you for your concern, but I assure you I shall be fine." Alyona left the house still fuming. That woman was insufferable.

She made it about half a versta before she turned her curricle around. Lev was correct: He had made his own life's decisions, and she was going to make hers. She strode into the house and told Cook to prepare some food for her to carry.

Cook nodded with satisfaction. "Good for you, mistress."

"I am not going to sneak out of here without telling him, though. I am going to do it openly. Where is my husband?"

"I have not seen him since breakfast."

"I shall go find him." She made her way through the house and heard the sound of movement coming from upstairs. She went to her room and found it empty, but voices and laughter resounded from Oksana's room. Certainly she knew where Lev had gone.

Alyona knocked twice as she swung the door open. There, she saw two people in the bed—one of them, her husband.

Oksana quickly sat up and pulled the sheet to cover her breasts. Lev rolled over lazily, as if this were just another normal morning. He stretched his arm behind his head. "I thought you were going to see your favorite convicts. We weren't expecting you back so soon."

"Clearly you were not." She looked at Oksana. "Get out of my house."

"You do not have the authority to order her out. She is my guest, and I say she stays."

"She may be *your* guest, but this is *my* house. The empress gave it to me specifically. I own it outright and I will say who is allowed here. You, Madame Tverskoya, are no longer welcome. I will, however, show you more respect than you have shown me. I will allow you one half hour to get yourself dressed. After that time, I will see to it that you are thrown out, clothed or not." She slammed the door behind her.

Lev followed her out in the hallway. He shoved her up against the wall. "You are my wife. You will do as I say."

"I wish you well in your efforts to make that happen, sir, but I can promise you they will not be successful. Put your pants on, get your trollop, and get out of my house. Be advised that she may never again trespass here. Not while there is life in my body."

"I pray that will not be long." He leaned closer, his face so red Alyona thought he might pass out. "I don't know why that wretched doctor spent so much effort to save you, when it was clear that any chance of your usefulness died along with the child." He shoved her aside and stormed back down the hallway.

Alyona slid to the floor, crushed beneath the weight of his venom. When she was finally able to draw breath, she forced herself to her feet. She would not give them the satisfaction of seeing her broken.

Within moments, Oksana's maid was summoned, trunks were packed, and the carriage brought around. Lev, too, packed his things. "Be informed, you cannot banish me from my own house. However, given the abysmal company here, I choose to go elsewhere for the time being."

Alyona watched them go and waited until they were out of sight before she returned to the house and cried. Whether the tears were because of hurt or anger or relief, she couldn't really say for sure.

CHAPTER 18

July, 1762

For the next few months, Alyona lived in a state of dread. She knew she had not heard the last of what had happened and supposed that Lev was biding his time until he came home and proved to her that he was, after all, in charge. She continued to correspond with Sophie, thankful for news from the outside world.

> *Dearest Sophie,*
> *How are you getting along? It must be difficult for you with all the changes.*
> *Can you tell me anything about what is happening in the city? I have heard dreadful rumors about the tsar's plans for his wife. I hope they are just rumors, but I fear for her.*
> *A*

> *Dearest Alyona,*
> *Things are quite unsettled here, but I remain hopeful for the future of our dear motherland. Only time will tell. I will write again*

when I know more.

S

One particularly beautiful day in July, Alyona was working in her little flower garden beside the house. Tikhon came from the barn, hand shading his eyes against the sun. "There is a rider coming up our driveway."

Alyona smiled in spite of herself. She suspected it was Viktor coming to check on their crops. His help had continued to prove invaluable over these past years. But as the horse drew closer and the rider came into clearer view, she grew alarmed. Dirty and bedraggled, the man dropped from his horse and handed the reins to Tikhon. Only then did she recognize him. "Lev." She ran to him. "Are you ill?"

He stared at the ground between them. "There has been a coup." His voice sounded gravelly, and his eyes were puffy and bloodshot.

"A coup? By whom?"

"Catherine. The Preobrazhensky Guards, led by the Orlov brothers, have deposed Tsar Peter and put Catherine on the throne."

"Catherine? But she is not even Russian born. Can this be true?"

"Yes." Lev nodded solemnly. "She rode through the streets in a guard's uniform, being cheered by the entire city. The whole lot declared their loyalty to her."

"What of Tsar Peter?"

"He has signed papers withdrawing himself as tsar and handing the power over to her. They are saying he will be sent to exile, but I will be surprised if he lives that long." He pulled at the back of his neck. "I must stay here and out of sight. It is a well-known fact that I was friends with Empress Elizabeth, as well as Peter and Elizaveta. Aside from that, Catherine has never liked me. If she is looking for people on whom to exact revenge, I need to make certain that she does not think of me."

The hair stood up on the back of Alyona's neck. The absolute power of the monarch ensured that a desire for revenge could destroy many lives. Empress Elizabeth had demonstrated this many times during her reign, with floggings, banishment, and worse. Lev's disfavor endangered their entire household.

Lev,

Tsar Peter III is dead. The palace has stated the cause as "hemor-rhoidal colic." We all know that he died at the hands of the Orlov brothers. I believe you should stay out of sight for the time being, my friend. Who knows what that woman shall do now that she has all the power? She has never favored you, as you are well aware.

Stay safe,
Pierre

Dearest Alyona,

Have you heard of the coup? It was quite thrilling. They awoke the grand duchess in the dead of night and told her that the coup was underway and she must come immediately. They left the Peterhof Palace in such a rush, she had her hair styled in the carriage on the way to the Winter Palace. Her husband, who was at the Oranien-baum Palace, never had an inkling until it was over and done. By the time the grand duchess arrived in St. Petersburg, there were fourteen thousand guards marching with her shouting, "hoorah." It was all so glorious. Everyone here is very happy.

Yours,

Sophie

As summer progressed, it became apparent that the normal rains were absent this year. It was as if the clouds sensed the upheaval beneath them and feared to release their precious drops to fall into it. Then the frost arrived early, killing much of what was left. Their barns remained half empty after the harvest.

One morning during breakfast, Cook came into the dining room. "Mistress, I need to see you for a moment please."

Lev folded his arms across his chest. "If it's another one of her beggars at the door, send him away and tell him we will scarce be able to feed ourselves this year."

Alyona cast a sharp glance toward her husband. "Here, Cook, please extend my breakfast to our visitor. I have not much of an appetite this morning."

"I told you I will not feed them with my food."

"This was *my* food. It was on my plate for my breakfast. If I choose not to eat it, what is that to you?"

"If you please," Cook never spoke so formally except when Lev was around, "this particular guest needs your special attention."

"Of course." Alyona stood and went with Cook.

"Do not give a thing. Not one thing." Lev's voice followed them out of the room, but he did not.

Once in the kitchen, Alyona saw the waif sitting at the table. Skinny and filthy, and not more than fifteen by the look of it. She kept her eyes trained on the floor when Alyona entered. "Are you all right?"

The girl shrugged and kept her eyes down. Cook handed Alyona a letter. "This came with her."

Dearest Alyona,

I hate to impose on your hospitality, but this poor wretch is pregnant with the child of a man who has been sent away from our country. Her father kicked her out of her home, and she was found living on the streets near starvation. I do not need to tell you that winter would have been the end of her. She needs somewhere safe to stay outside the city for a few weeks until I can finalize other arrangements. I would keep her with me if it were possible, but I cannot. I have enclosed five rubles to cover expenses. I know this is a disruption, but you are the only person I can trust to keep her safe. I will send for her as soon as possible. Her name is Galina. Please treat her with the same kindness you have always extended to me.

Your friend,

Sophie

"Oh, you poor thing." Alyona set her plate down in front of the girl. "Please, eat. I will go see that your room is made ready."

Cook followed Alyona out of the kitchen and whispered, "I can keep her at my house."

Alyona shook her head. "No. I will put her in our nicest guest room. Since Sophie has tasked me with keeping her safe, I will be the one to see to it. If I put her in the same room where my husband was once found with his mistress, perhaps it will help erase my memories of that awful moment and replace them with something better."

"Will the count agree with this?"

"Most certainly not. But no matter. He should look at it as a chance for atonement."

When she went to tell her husband about the new plans, he

had already left the breakfast table. She searched throughout the house and did not find him, but when she went into his study, she saw that two new pieces of mail had arrived for him. She picked them up and saw they came from St. Petersburg.

Please be advised that you are no longer considered a necessary expense of the imperial government and are herewith stripped of all such charities. Your stipend is heretofore permanently revoked.

While this was not a surprise, the finality of it made it feel all the more real. This information had likely sent Lev out for the day, in the hopes of relief in cards and vodka.

Then she opened the second letter. It was short—clearly written by someone hired to write for an illiterate patron.

This is to inform you that Oksana Tverskoya and her child are healthy and doing well. Congratulations on the birth of your son.

CHAPTER 19

*L*ev did not return home until late that night. As Alyona had expected, he was drunk. He climbed into bed, muttering under his breath about women and their general lack of worth. Though she kept her eyes shut, he ranted and raved and ranted some more. "Worthless, all of you, worthless." Finally, the words ceased, replaced by snores.

Alyona and Galina were already halfway through their breakfast the next morning before Lev came down the stairs. He took one look at the sickly girl dressed in rags and roared, "What is *this* doing at my breakfast table?"

"Dearest." Alyona took care to use her calmest voice. "This is Galina. She will be staying with us for a couple of weeks."

"She most certainly will not." He pointed his finger at Galina. "Get out of my house this very instant."

Galina stood but so did Alyona. "Sit down, please, Galina. You are most welcome here." She squared her shoulders and stared at her husband. "My friend Sophie sent her to me and asked me to care for her until final arrangements can be made for her travel." She continued to look at him evenly, refusing to show any trace of fear or doubt, although she had plenty of both. It was clear from his puffy and bloodshot eyes that he was quite hungover from yesterday's adventures. He rarely had the will to fight at times like this, and she hoped that to be the case today.

"That servant girl Sophie? Why is my wife taking orders from a servant?"

"Not orders. It was a request." Alyona did not tell him about the money. When she sent Galina on her way, she had every intention of sending that money with her to help her get started in her new life. If Lev knew of its existence, that would never happen.

"Well, then I *request* that you get her out of here."

"You are being rude to our guest. As I said, she will only be here for a couple of weeks, but I have every intention of extending hospitality to her for as long as necessary."

"Then she can stay with the servants and eat breakfast with them."

"She is staying in the east guest room." Alyona looked at him and let it sink in exactly which room that was. "She will be made as comfortable as possible there and will eat at this table. You most certainly are welcome to take your meals elsewhere if this makes you uncomfortable. As you remember, dearest, this is *my* house."

"Please, madame, I—"

Alyona held out her hand to stop Galina from finishing her sentence. "You are welcome here. We have had other guests in that same room recently with much poorer manners than yours. It will be nice to have someone in our home who is pleasant for a change."

Lev grabbed the back of his chair and slammed it to the floor. He stormed out the front door without another word.

ALYONA HUGGED GALINA GOOD-BYE. "BEST WISHES ON your new life."

"Thank you, Countess. I do not know what I would have done without you." In truth, Alyona had taken great pains to see that Galina ate nutritious foods, rested, and took short walks to regain her strength. Two weeks later, her health had much improved.

"I am thankful you did not have to find out. Please, after you are settled, send word that you have arrived safely."

Galina nodded as she climbed into the carriage, but Alyona doubted she would hear from the girl again. She prayed that the family who was taking her in would be kind to her.

As she watched the carriage depart, she tried in vain to tamp down her outrage at the unfairness of it all. Galina pregnant with an unwanted child that almost cost her life, Oksana birthing a healthy son out of wedlock. *Why, God? Why them and not me?*

Cook came to stand beside her on the driveway. "Did you find out anything about the father?"

Alyona sighed. "Not much. Trying to get Galina to speak was quite a chore. I surmised that he played some part in the coup, for which side I do not know. His family thought it best to send him out of the country to attend school while things settled down."

"So, there is no prospect that he will marry her?"

"It does not appear so. Her father is a peasant and had betrothed her to a much older man whom she despised. She met a young man and fell in love, and he with her, or at least so she believes. I gather that his family was of some rank, because she did not believe marriage would have been allowed, even if they knew of the child."

When Alyona made her way inside, she found Lev already seated at the lunch table. "We will not have enough money to make it through the winter. We are going to have to relieve most of the hired hands."

"No." Alyona shook her head. "We cannot do that."

"We have no choice."

"We can cut back our own spending until next year's harvest. Those people need their jobs much more than we need to heat this large house. We can condense into a few rooms during the winter. We can cut our portions of food. It might not be pleasant, but it will see us through until next summer when, God willing, the rains will return and the harvest will be plentiful.

"I will not live like a pauper."

"That seems to be our only choice."

"We shall see about that." He went into his study and slammed the door behind him. An hour later he placed a letter in Tikhon's hands. "Deliver this at once and wait for a response."

"Yes, Your Excellency."

It was late that night before Tikhon returned. Lev opened the parcel and smiled. "Our financial future is secure."

"What has happened?"

"Madame Tverskoya has agreed to purchase all my land surrounding the estate."

"You cannot be serious? If she purchases all that land, how will the estate remain self-sustaining?"

"There is a small parcel that came with your house. That should keep you fed. As for the farmhands, they are now at Madame Tverskoya's disposal." He looked at her and cocked his eyebrow. "I know they are all great friends of yours. Perhaps you might want to tell them to begin searching for other places of employment." He gestured for one of the maids. "Summon Pavel and tell him to pack my trunks at once. I will depart this very night."

"Where are you going?"

"St. Petersburg. I will live in the home with my son—since you have refused to provide me one."

The blow fell with every bit of pain he had intended. It took all of her strength to stay upright.

Less than an hour later his carriage pulled away from their house. What was to become of them all? How was Alyona to provide for everyone?

She did not know, but she vowed to find a way.

Even though...I will...because You.

CHAPTER 20

"*P*lease spread the word that there will be a Christmas Feast this year. At my table. For all who wish to come." Alyona kept her spine straight, shoulders back, hoping she appeared more confident than she felt.

Cook continued to stir the pot of stew in a show of nonchalance, but Alyona saw her right eye twitch. "And what if the count should make his annual appearance?"

"Then he shall see that I am making my own decisions, based on what I believe is right. And will no longer by constrained by his whim." She lifted her chin a fraction of an inch. "Nor will I allow him to order the people I love away from my table."

Cook inhaled deeply, her spoon slowing its circuit. Finally, she nodded. "God be with you, mistress." She set the spoon aside and walked over to place her hands on Alyona's shoulders. "You can count on my support."

Alyona could have collapsed with relief. She needed this confirmation more than she had realized. "Thank you, Cook."

ON CHRISTMAS EVE, ALYONA AND COOK PREPARED for the usual visitors. "This year's offerings will be meager. I fear that I will not adequately show appreciation to the household."

"You always provide the best you are able. This year, this is your best."

"But it's not enough. All has been lost."

Cook took Alyona's hands between her own. "All is not lost. Just because you can't do everything does not mean you can not do anything. The child who provided the loaves and the fishes gave what he had—certainly not enough to feed the multitudes, but he willingly gave all that he was able. The Lord did the blessing and because of that, thousands of people were fed, but it all began with that small gift of faith. You continue to do what you can and trust that the Lord can bless your small offering as well."

But what could God do to fix this? Alyona had no loaves or fishes to offer.

Every little while, there would be a knock at the back door. Often stragglers asking for a piece of bread. Alyona brought each and every one of them into the kitchen, put some bread on a plate before them, and invited them back for tomorrow's Christmas feast.

Then the neighbors started dropping by. A few at first and then more. Instead of the usual Christmas Eve visitation, this time they brought food. "Just something to add to the table tomorrow," they said over and over.

Dmitri and his wife came, pulling a wagon full. "When I was out making my morning rounds, people asked me to send this along."

Alyona looked at Cook. "We cannot allow this to continue. These people need this food to hold them over through the winter."

Cook put her face very close to hers. "As do you. They are simply giving what they have—just as you have been doing."

"I feel wrong taking it."

"I suspect they, too, feel wrong taking tomorrow's feast from you. You must let them give as their conscience dictates."

Dmitri looked at her. "Oh, mistress, what I would not give to see you get the kind of gift that you deserve for Christmas."

"Dmitri, I could not think of anything better than what I am receiving now in the love and generosity of those around me."

She meant every word of it.

IT WAS WELL BEFORE DAWN ON CHRISTMAS MORNING when a pounding at the door awakened Alyona. Since she had made herself a pallet in the parlor to avoid heating the upstairs, she wrapped herself in a shawl and hurried to the door. A courier stood there, his cloak covered in snow. "Urgent letter for the Countess Vorontsova."

"That is I. Please come in and warm yourself." Alyona led the man into the dining room. He glanced at the blankets and pillow where she'd been sleeping near the stove but said nothing. Alyona supposed she should be embarrassed, but she was well past that now.

Alyona,
You must come to St. Petersburg immediately. The empress has
summoned us to meet her at the Winter Palace at 10:00 a.m.
Wear your nicest dress and be prepared to beg forgiveness for

whatever infraction of which we are about to be accused. I am staying at the home of Madame Tverskoya. Call for me here as soon as you arrive.

Cook came into the parlor. "Who was at the door?" She saw the man near the stove, then cast a worried gaze upon Alyona.

"Will you help me get dressed?" Alyona handed her the letter, still in a daze.

Cook made clucking sounds as she read. "Of course I will help you. First, I will awaken Tikhon and tell him to prepare the troika for your journey."

Alyona turned toward the courier still shivering by the stove. "I will see that you have some hot tea and a warm breakfast soon."

"Thank you, madame."

As quickly as possible, she was dressed and bundled in the troika. Cook was still making clucking sounds. "I wish the master had not taken the vozok with him to St. Petersburg. You will be frozen clear through by the time you arrive."

As this was true, there was no need to argue it. "Yes, but so is the poor courier who had much less at stake than I do during this journey. Please see to it that he is well fed and given somewhere to rest and that his horse is also well tended."

"Of course."

"And please, continue with the Christmas feast as planned."

"We couldn't possibly."

"Of course you can and you must. The food is all prepared. The neighbors have been most generous. Not a single morsel is to go to waste, do you understand me? I will send word if I am able and let you know of our circumstance."

"We will all be praying for you."

"What better time to be prayed for than on the glorious morning we celebrate the birth of our Savior?" Alyona reached out and squeezed Cook's hand. "No matter what happens, please know how much I love you and value every single member of this household. Please...make certain they all know that."

"They know already, but I will tell them once again."

"Thank you, dear friend." And with that, Alyona began the journey toward whatever destiny awaited her.

CHAPTER 21

*a*s the troika pulled up to Madame Tverskoya's mansion, Alyona battled a new bout of anger. Lev lived so fine here in St. Petersburg, while his household in Taitsy rationed food and heating fuel. *Why?*

Lev came outside as soon as the troika arrived. "It is good that you are on time."

"I do not believe there is much choice in cases such as this. What is it all about?"

He shook his head. "I have no idea. Catherine has never liked me, but I can think of nothing I have done that might anger her. There were many who were closer than I to her former husband, and most of them have suffered no ill effects."

It was only a short distance to the Winter Palace, so they arrived quickly. The Christmas candles flickered through the frost-covered windows as the inhabitants prepared for their day of feasting and celebration. Just another blessed Christmas morn, without concerns of prison, or exile, or revenge. How Alyona envied that kind of peace.

Once inside, a maid led them to a small parlor. "Wait here, please. Her Imperial Majesty will be with you soon."

The two of them stood side by side in silence. Time passed, and Lev began to pace. Over an hour later, Alyona took an uneasy seat on an embroidered chair. Had they been forgotten?

At length, a maid arrived and set out tea and a display of delicacies. Dark hair peeked out from her white cap, framing perfect ivory skin. Her posture was perfect to the point of rigidity. She approached Alyona and whispered, "You are Sophie's friend, are you not?"

"I am. Is she here?"

"She is elsewhere in the palace, but she wanted me to tell you something."

"Yes?"

"Galina, the young girl she sent to you, has died."

"No." Alyona put her hand over her mouth. "That poor, sweet, darling girl."

"Yes, the childbirth was long and difficult. The baby, however, survived. One of Galina's dying wishes was for you to raise her daughter. Sophie wants to know if you would be willing to do that?"

Lev was already shaking his head. "Absolutely not."

Alyona looked toward the girl again and said, "I am honored that she would trust me with her child. At present, however, we are waiting for a meeting with Her Imperial Majesty, and I am not certain what that will mean for us."

"But if you are to return home, you would accept the child?"

"I would accept her and love her with all my heart."

The maid curtsied and returned to her task.

Lev rounded on Alyona. "I will not allow some peasant's illegitimate child to live in my household."

"You yourself do not live in that household and have not for many years. You parade around your mansion with your own illegitimate child, leaving us all to fend for ourselves. As I have said before, the house is mine. I shall determine who lives there and who does not."

"You will not get one extra ruble from me. All it will do is take food out of the mouths of the servants and peasants you love so well."

"That child will be provided for in my house for as long as I am able."

The maid shuffled from the room, looking equal parts embarrassed and enthralled with the conversation she had just overheard. Alyona dropped into the chair, determined to say no more on the subject.

After a while, the door opened again and in walked a woman with intricately braided dark-brown hair, wearing an exquisite white velvet gown and ropes and ropes of pearls. Beside her was a giant of a man wearing the uniform of the Preobrazhensky Guards. Alyona could only assume this was the Empress Catherine and her favorite, Grigory Orlov.

Alyona stood, curtsied deeply, and out of the corner of her eye could see Lev bowing beside her.

"A blessed Christmas morning to you," the empress said.

Alyona was trembling. As much as she and Lev were at odds, she did not want something bad to happen to him. Nor did she want to be included in his downfall. She kept her eyes downcast, waiting to hear the accusations that were sure to come.

The silence drew on longer and longer. Would Alyona's legs continue to hold her upright for much longer? She finally raised her gaze, mostly because she wanted to see what the empress was doing in this long silence. She was staring directly at Alyona.

"Do you not recognize your old friend?"

"Your Imperial Majesty?" The words came out shaky.

"You truly do not recognize me?"

"I do humbly apologize, but I can remember no meeting between us."

"Oh, but there was one." Her voice did have a slightly familiar tone, but nothing about her looked familiar. Except...

the pointy chin, the startling blue eyes. It couldn't be... "Sophie?" Alyona gasped. "The young servant whose child had just died?"

"So you believed me to be, when you spent hours tending to my needs when all else had abandoned me."

"But..." Alyona shook her head, trying to make sense of it all. "You told me...you told me that your son had died."

"No. I said my son had been taken from me. You assumed."

"I...I suppose that I did."

"And so he was...taken from me. For the past eight years I have had to beg and plead to even be afforded the occasional glimpse of my own child."

"I am sorry, Your Imperial Majesty. I did not know to whom I was speaking until this very moment."

She nodded. "And yet you wrote me letters, spoke kindly to me, and even took in the wayward girl whom I sent to you just a few months ago, without ever expecting to receive anything in return." The empress pointed toward the door through which the maid had gone. "And when I sent in one of my closest ladies-in-waiting, disguised as a maid and asked if you would take care of the child, you immediately agreed to offer her not only shelter but love." She glanced toward Lev. "In spite of what it was going to cost you."

Lev had gone full white. "Forgive me, Your Imperial Majesty, I did not mean—"

"Save your foul breath for someone who would believe the words you vomit." She turned back toward the man in uniform then and motioned for him to speak.

"My name is Grigory Orlov. The child's father is my younger brother, Vladimir. We sent him away after the coup because he is impetuous and young. He did not know about the child. I, myself, only learned of the situation after the girl was found starving on the streets.

"So, we concocted a story of a husband dead from small pox

and sent her to a safe place to raise her child without shame. Unfortunately, as you have heard, she did not survive." He walked over and took Alyona's hand, looking her full in the face. "In this short time, I have heard enough to know you would be the perfect mother for this child. I only ask one thing. My brother can never know. If he were to find out about any of it, his quick temper would guarantee the death of Galina's parents —as well as anyone else whom he might decide to blame. Many lives would be destroyed."

"Yes," the empress said, "in fact, the story must be told that this is your own child. By birth."

"But, Your Majesty, my miscarriage many years ago left me unable to bear a child. Many people know this."

"Doctors can be wrong, can they not?"

Alyona nodded. "I suppose...for my part, I shall keep the secret as you have asked."

"That is all I ask." Catherine turned toward Lev. "As for you, your current life is no secret to me, nor to anyone else in the city. You will indeed cover the cost for this child to live and thrive. Do not be mistaken. I will see to it that you do. In fact, I had planned to offer a stipend to cover expenses, but hearing of the things you just said to your wife about not giving one ruble... well, I shall see to it that you are made a liar. The child is your financial responsibility from this moment forward."

Lev nodded, his face white. "As you wish."

The empress turned back to Alyona. "As for you, you befriended me and helped me when, as far as you knew, there was nothing beneficial I could do in return. Now, I ask you, what would you like for me to do for you? I would be happy to provide you a home here at the palace. You would be well tended and cared for, and the child provided every luxury."

Alyona shook her head. "I thank you for the kind offer, Your Majesty, but I am happy in Taitsy. However, there is one problem I have, for which I beg your assistance."

"Name it."

"When my husband and I married, we hired many of the servants from my father's estate in Kazan." She took a breath. "Our land has recently been sold, and I believe it is possible that many will lose their employment. I know that you, too, are against the practice of serfdom. Would you be willing to hire them to work on one of your estates?"

The empress cut her eyes toward Lev. "I have heard of the land purchase of which you speak. While I would like to give the land in its entirety over to you, that would not be following the laws of our land. I can, however, make absolutely certain that the new landowner not only keeps every single one in her employ, I will see that she increases their pay." She glared at Lev. "I do not see any problem with this, do you, Count Vorontsov?"

It was plain from his expression that he did very much expect there to be a problem with this. He also knew there was no other choice. "I am certain the new landowner would be honored that you take such a personal interest in her land, Your Majesty."

"As I thought." She nodded toward Alyona. "And now, may I present you with a special gift for this blessed day." She gestured toward a footman, who opened a side door.

And there she was. The "maid" from earlier carried in the tiny child, wrapped in a thick white blanket. She handed the bundle to Alyona, a huge smile on her face.

"She already has a wet nurse who will live with you and help care for the child." Catherine cast a pointed look at Lev. "She, too, will be paid by you, Count Vorontsov. I believe the recent sale of your land should provide you plenty of rubles to spare." Then she turned back to Alyona. "I have seen that you were outfitted with all the necessities since you could have in no way been prepared."

The empress started through the door and then turned. "I

look forward to continued letters from you, and this time, I expect to hear all about your new baby."

"I look forward to writing those, if you are still willing to receive them, Your Majesty."

"Most willing. And please, continue to address them to Sophie. You alone loved me for who I was and not what I was. I want to be reminded of that always." She swept from the room then, but not before she gave Grigory Orlov a meaningful look.

As soon as she was gone, the huge man barreled toward Lev and pulled him up by the shirt until their faces almost touched. "If I should hear that you are spreading even one little hint about this child's parentage, I will see to it that you are never again able to father a child. And that will be the least of your problems. Do you understand me?"

"Yes." Lev choked out the word.

"Good. Make certain that Tverskoya tramp understands it, too."

"Of course." Lev's face was glowing bright red—from anger or lack of air, Alyona did not know.

"You are not worthy of the lady at your side." With that, Grigory shoved him away, and Lev fell, hitting his head against the wall on his way down. Grigory turned to Alyona, picked up her hand, and kissed it. "It is an honor to know you. I wish you all the best with your new daughter."

He looked down at the sweet face in the bundle and touched her cheek. "She is beautiful. My brother, were he aware, would be most grateful to know that she is in loving hands like yours. I express thanks on his behalf." He bowed then and strutted out of the room.

CHAPTER 22

A footman entered the parlor and nodded toward Alyona. "I am told you made the trip today in a troika. Since it would not be safe to carry the infant such a long distance in the frigid air, the empress has made other arrangements. Her personal vozok is being prepared now. You, sir—" he bowed toward Lev— "are to come with me."

Lev stood and rubbed the back of his head. He came up close to Alyona and growled low and furious. "She is not my daughter, nor will she ever be." He followed the footman out the door.

Soon after, Lidia, the wet nurse arrived. She appeared to be quite young, with small, dark eyes open wide in fear. Alyona put her hand on the woman's arm. "If you are a wet nurse, then you have a child of your own?"

Lidia sniffled. "My baby died after she was born."

"And...do you have other children?"

"No." She sniffled again. "I was only married last year."

"I see. And your husband, what of him?"

She shrugged. "He will remain here in the city, as he is a valet for the tsarevich."

"Oh, I see." Alyona knew that this advantageous position

was not one he would want to leave behind. She also understood that for the foreseeable future, Lidia's presence would be required near the baby. "Please, tell your husband that he will always have a welcome place to stay in our home. He may visit at any time."

Lidia's eyes grew wide. "I have never heard of such kindness."

The footman returned. "Your vozok is waiting out front."

"My husband?"

"I believe he was sent home on foot. Your troika will be returned to your estate by tomorrow's end, after the horses have had time to rest."

"I thank you." The footman escorted the two women out to their conveyance where they climbed inside, finding that the vozok had been fully warmed before their arrival. Two large trunks were attached to the back, so Alyona knew that the empress—Sophie—had indeed provided for the child. She gazed down at the baby, then back at Lidia. "Does she have a name?"

"Her mother named her Valentina before she died. It means strength and power. Of course, she is but an infant and you are starting her out new. You could change the name and no one would be the wiser."

Alyona shook her head. "I think this little one will be a tower of strength. I cannot think of a better name." And with that, the little trio began their journey home.

SEVERAL HOURS LATER, WHEN THE VOZOK PULLED UP in front of her home, Alyona thought of the people who were inside celebrating the Christmas feast. Could she trust them to keep the secret?

She turned to Lidia who was currently feeding the baby. "Please stay here with Valentina for a few minutes. Let me go explain to our visitors what has happened, and then I will send for you."

Lidia nodded. "Do not worry about us. It is warm and dry in here, and Mistress Valentina is enjoying her meal."

Alyona made her way toward the front door, rehearsing the words she had practiced in the carriage. The door flung open and Cook's eyes grew wide at the fancy vozok. "Mistress, is everything all right?" She hurried Alyona inside. "Please, you must tell us everything."

It was then that Alyona noticed the silence of the house. She had expected conversation and laughter, but there was nothing. "Where is everyone?"

Cook pointed into the parlor, where dozens of her friends and neighbors assembled. Most were on their knees, all were facing the icon corner with candles lit. "No one felt much like celebrating this morning; we were all so worried about you. So we turned it into a time of prayer instead."

One by one the people rose from their knees, the worry obvious on their faces. Alyona thought she might die for the love she felt at this moment, for all them. "Please, everyone be seated. All is well, but I have something to tell you."

They exchanged nervous glances but quickly settled. Waiting.

"Do you remember the young girl Galina who stayed with us?" And she told them the entire story. "I must ask all of you to do your best to keep this secret with me; otherwise, it could mean trouble."

They all nodded, but no one said a word. This was not a group of people who practiced untruth; it went against their natures. A few throats cleared, there was a cough, an uncomfortable shifting.

Alyona took a deep breath. "One minute. I will present her

to you." Alyona made her way out to the carriage. Lidia handed her the baby, then followed her inside, where the assembled group sat staring.

"I would like to present Lidia, our new nurse. Her husband will remain in St. Petersburg where he works in service of the tsarevich. I know that you will all show her every kindness." Alyona turned and lifted her left elbow so Valentina's face was aimed toward the crowd. "And may I introduce my daughter, Valentina Lvovna Vorontsova."

"She is beautiful," came a woman's voice. "Such a darling little thing," said another.

Then Dmitri stood and put his hand over his heart. "I remember back when you were in a family way with her. How you used to get so sick in the mornings. We thought there for a while she would be the death of you."

The room was silent for a moment, then Katya, the midwife also stood. "I remember the shock of finding you were with child, after I had wrongly believed that impossible. And such a blessing the delivery went so well."

"Yes, such a rosy-cheeked glow you had while carrying the child." "Yes, just lovely." Each contributed his or her part of the story. Sonya stood and said, "Countess Vorontsova, I pledge you my oath that from this day forward, not a soul shall hear any story about this child other than the one shared here."

Everyone agreed, and Alyona thought her heart might burst with joy. She turned to Cook. "Now that everyone's prayers have been answered, mine most of all, I think it is time we serve up the Christmas feast and share together in the joy of our Savior's birth, as well as the joy of this new little life in our midst."

"Here, here," Dmitri said.

"Here, here," came shouts from around the room.

And for the rest of the day and well into the night, that's exactly what they did.

Late that night, after Alyona tucked Valentina snugly into her crib, she made her way down the stairs and fell on her knees at the icon corner.

"Father, thank You. You were true to Your word all along, even when I could not see You.

"Even though...I will...because You. And I will, Father, for the rest of my life. Because You are there. Always."

QUESTIONS FOR CONVERSATION

1) Alyona believed that everything would be fine if she could just have a child. Do you think a child would have made a difference in her marriage? Can you relate to the "if only _____ then my life would be great"?

2) Alyona's "shunning" made her private sadness all the more painful, and public. Do you feel that women without children are seen as less-than in today's society? Or unmarried women? Some other group?

3) Lev truly seemed to want to be a good husband at times during this story. Do you think a child early on would have helped him achieve that? Do you think it was possible for him to be the man he originally vowed to try to be, or was his nature too self-centered?

4) Alyona looked around the table and wondered what her life might have been like if she had married Viktor. Do you ever wonder what your life would have been like if you had made a different choice at some junction? Are those kinds of thoughts helpful or dangerous?

5) Alyona struggled with the unfairness, the "why." Do you find yourself asking "why"?

6) Alyona's relationship with Lev is complicated. She wants to please him, and obviously longs for him to be at home and living as a responsible husband, yet she often feels relieved after he departs. Do you believe she loves him, or is this just self-preservation?

7) Were you surprised to learn the identity of Sophie? (Catherine's birth name was Sophie of Anhalt-Zerbst. It was changed to Catherine when she converted to Russian Orthodoxy before marrying Grand Duke Peter). Do you think Alyona should have taken her offer of life at the palace?

8) When Alyona returned with Valentina, she explained to her assembled friends and neighbors the story that needed to be told of Valentina's birth. At first, everyone remained silent because "this was not a group of people who practiced untruth; it went against their natures." Do you think it was wrong to ask them to perpetuate a story they knew to be untrue? Was it wrong for Alyona to tell the same untrue story?

ACKNOWLEDGMENTS

Lee, Melanie, and Caroline Cushman- Every single day I am grateful that I get to be part of such an amazing family. Also, thanks for accompanying me on my dream trip around the Baltic Sea, which spawned the desire to write historical fiction in Imperial Russia. Thanks for humoring me in my dinner dissertations about Russian history, my online Russian language classes, and the Russian folk music blasting through the house while I'm writing.

SAFS book club- Stacey, Rachel, Jamie, Kat, and Emily—What a privilege to speak monthly with friends from multiple countries who share a love of reading and Russian history. You are an amazing group of women. I hope we all meet in person someday.

Kathleen—For being a true friend, wise advisor, and fun travel buddy.

Alisa Parrish- Your strength and courage have always inspired me, never more than this year. You are a true hero in every sense of the word.

Carl Parrish- for being an encourager, friend, helper, and almost exact approximation of Pops (the praise could not get any higher than this).

Judy and Denice- our little zoom Bible study group has been such a blessing over the past couple of years. Thank you for keeping me grounded.

Brenna, Lisa, and Susie- A bedrock of friendship, and great pickleball partners too.

Mike and Lisa Champion- stalwart friends through life's hard times.

Lisa Cushman- our daily check-ins have solved so many of the world's problems —if only the world would listen to us. Thanks for your encouragement.

The Goodland Book Club- Genessa, Shannon, Christy, Nikki, Christine, Leora, Cindy, Keely, Amy, Nancy, and Robyn. Thank you for loving the written word as much as I do, and reminding me why I do this. What an amazing group of women you are.

Julee Schwarzburg- Thank you making the big picture so much clearer in these stories.

Carrie Padgett- For cleaning up the final product, offering encouragement, and generally being a lifelong friend.

Stacey Watson- Thank you for reading through the manuscript and helping make it more authentically Russian.

Torrey Lind- For designing the little vozok and troika to separate the scenes. Thanks for taking my random ideas and turning them into exactly what I need.

ACKNOWLEDGMENTS

Most of all- thank You Heavenly Father for carrying me through those times when it has seemed impossible to take one more step forward on my own.

ALSO BY KATHRYN CUSHMAN

A Promise to Remember

Waiting for Daybreak

Leaving Yesterday

Another Dawn

Chasing Hope

Almost Amish

Finding Me

Fading Starlight

By Kathryn Cushman and Lauren Beccue

The Plans We Made

By Kathryn Cushman and Sheila Walsh

Angel Song